Unhallowed

by

D.P. Pankratz

Don. P. Pankratz

Copyright © 2018 D.P. Pankratz

Printed in the United States by Lulu. Com

LIBRARY AND ARCHEIVES CANADA CATALOGING-IN PUBLICATION DATA

Pankratz, Don. P (Don. P. P.)

Unhallowed/Don. P. Pankratz

ISBN 978-1-9994821-0-7

Printed in the United States of America

Lulu. Com

Second Edition

Book cover design, Zoe Hudon

Unhallowed

<u>Dedications</u>

To my wife Teresa, you've stood with me in the darkness, and into the light. Twenty-eight years together, and you still put up with my "quirks." With heart felt joy, I dedicate this book to you!

A great big Thank you to my editor, Sam Stinn! I'm forever indebted to you, without your skills and abilities, I would be lost at sea… thank you from the bottom of my heart.

Thank you Terry Hoet, a friend who has help me greatly accomplish getting Unhallowed out into public. You my friend are one of a kind, and I'm honored to know you.

I would like to also thank all the people who stood by me in my time of need. There are too many to thank individually, but I'm sure you know who you are, so thank you all!

TABLE OF CONTENTS

Don. P. Pankratz

<u>TABLE OF CONTENTS CONTD</u>

Somewhere deep in the Rainforest…

This being our third trip to the spirit village since first coming here in 1879… June 12, my party and I make our way through the ghastly overgrowth and whatever dangers lay below. It's been twenty-eight days of blistering heat, and we've lost nine members to the many poisonous creatures. Finally, we see the outer outlines of the village, and I gain my first impression of the people, under a new chief, dressed as the dead: wearing the skins of other human beings like clothing. They still have a willow tree full of tiny coffins surrounded by forty decomposing bodies with a circular trench surrounding the bodies. The new interpreter tells us not to even look towards the tree but refuses to offer an explanation. The menacing look of fear on his face tells us this tree is purely something dark or evil and should never be disrespected. As my partner and the rest of the team stand outside of the village, watching and waiting for the chief to invite us within the salted circle that surrounds this mystical place, a heavily decorated man approaches my interpreter and myself.

This man speaks in his tribal tongue and stops to allow our interpreter to restate what he has said, "We are welcome to enter his village, but we must abide by their customs or suffer a fate worse than death itself!"

After agreeing to his terms, we all bow to him. Once he allows us inside the strange and mysterious village, I feel an ominous uneasiness about this place. My partner Kevin, after almost receiving a spear in the face for looking at the willow tree, falls to his knees and we realize they are serious about the willow tree. Watching Kevin slowly get to his feet with the spearhead still mere inches from his eye, I can only assume those decomposing corpses are of those who perhaps looked at what they should not have.

Kevin joins me again and whispers, "Damn that was close, but I did get a good look at the one casket, Edward!"

Giving him a glaring look, I mutter back, "Don't do anything to upset these people, we know nothing about them. Let's just wait and perhaps, in time, they will share their culture with us." Following them into a hut, we are stripped of our clothes and forced to our knees as a man dressed in black feathers walks in front of us. The smell of death lingers.

His eyes are blood red, and his voice is as dark as the devil himself as he states, "You come to my home… uninvited. You come here of all places…why?" He points to one of the villagers who helped us get here; the naked man shook as he said something in his native tongue. The man dressed in black feathers turns his eyes towards me and walks back my way, stopping nearby. As I look at the red of his eyes, wondering what's going to happen to us, he asks:

"Why...? Why did you choose here as your destination?"

He glares at me and my chest feels heavy, as if a loaded wagon were sitting atop of me. Gasping, I respond, "We came here to explore. Someone mentioned there was a long-lost village deep in the rainforest that held many secrets. We come in peace."

His glare would make the dead want to run. I look at his hand and see a maggot crawling into his finger. He answers, "Secrets... you came here for secrets? You are but a human. The only things you need to know is that from the moment you drop from your mothers, you are already in death's hands. You feed, only by my graces, and you die by my hand! Those are the ONLY things you need to know!"

I watch him as he steps in front of Kevin, and asks, "Did you also come here for these secrets?" His eyes focused on Kevin, as he kneeled down to eye level, waiting for Kevin to answer him.

Kevin finally looks up and replies, "I came for knowledge!"

The man wearing the black feathers stands up again, looking at each of us evilly as he answers, "One here for secrets, another here for knowledge... what about you?" he points to another villager, and the man breaks down and starts weeping.

He cries out, "I was paid to bring them here… please, I'm sorry," and places his head on the ground, begging. The one with the feathers grabs the man and lifts him into a standing position.

"Did you cry when you took the money to come here? NO! Did you take a second to reconsider coming here? NO! Your greed brought you here, and now you will learn why your fathers warned you to never come here!"

Our guide began to urinate as the man wearing the black feathers looks at him menacingly. A feeling of hate ravages over me. Trying to shake it off, I watch the glare become too much for the man and he bolts for the entrance, impaling himself on two spears. His body slumped over, making an eerie gurgling sound, and the one in black walked to a stone throne to sit down, staring at the remaining seven of us. Fearing our fate will be much the same as our guide, I take a breath and try again to speak, "Sir… there is much we can learn from each other…"

His eyes turn to me as he responds, "You dare speak when NOT spoken to? WHAT IS YOUR NAME?" Anticipating an answer, he angrily leaned forward.

"Edward Robinson… Sir!" I reply, as he stands up and walks over to me.

He puts his foot on my right leg and replies, "Edward Robinson… what is it you think I can learn from you, that I already don't know?"

Watching his eyes glare at me, I reply, "I don't know, but if we talk to each other, I'm sure we can find something?"

Laughing at the suggestion, he replies, "Alright... tell me about your wife Margret."

"She is a lovely woman; she is the love of my life."

Putting more weight on my leg, he replies, "Good... I hope nothing bad happens to her. I will make you an offer as you have one member of your group who does not follow the rules: You will place your wife's soul as your bond... break one of our rules again and she will be mine! Do I make myself clear as daylight?"

I looked over at Kevin, worried, and then back up at the man. "Yes. I swear we will not break any more rules," I reply as he removes his foot. Brushing maggots off my leg as he walks back to his throne, he turns and points to another man.

"You. What is your name?"

I lean forward enough to see he is pointing at Jack Roslyn.

"Jack Roslyn!"

The man smiles from the throne, "You are now welcome members of this village. Don't disrespect the rules or else..."

We watch as smoke covers the throne, and once it clears there is a man sitting there wearing a raven headdress, looking like the rest of the tribe. He stands and walks over to us.

"While here... you will obey the laws of our land!"

"Yes!" I reply as the others follow in line. He motions for us to rise with his hands, reaching towards the roof. As I stand up, I look at his eyes; he is still glaring, but they are less intrusive.

He states, "The rest of you stay here. I will take this man with me." He motions for me to walk. As we get outside of the hut, he starts up an ancient path covered with foliage. As we walk, he doesn't utter a word, and instead remains focused on wherever we're headed. He stops once we reach the top of a plateau, and my eyes wander around cautiously. A stone slab table, discolored and weathered, sits at the epicenter amidst three huge stone carvings of some sort of demon or God- like statues. Finally, he speaks:

"This right here is eternity… the one place where man and Gods meet. You are fortune that Abrazz accepted your request. Many men such as you meet with your fate here."

Listening to him closely, as his English is strained, I ask, "Who is this Abra--Abrazz?"

"Sit!" Looking at the ground as I sit on a rock, he stands in front of me, his eyes glossy in the greyish light of the day. "He is the mightiest of all Gods, he stands in the middle there… he commands the armies of the dead; his heart is of the pouring rains. He was exiled from Africa 5000 years ago from the underworld and came here, where he taught us a great many things, including the rules."

"May I ask about the tree, and why it is forbidden to look at it?" I ask as he squints at me.

"You should not even whisper that question. I will tell you this… disrespect the rules here, and you will find the true measure of Abrazz's wrath… never bring it up again!"

12

Unhallowed

"I am sorry… I meant no disrespect," I reply as he shakes his head.

He looks toward the stone carving and answers, "That is not up to me to decide… we should go back to your companions."

Getting up, he bows to the carvings and I nod, following his lead. He begins descending the path and, taking one last look at the menacing face looking back at me, I follow behind the chief.

"The tree prevents the demons from wreaking havoc amongst the living, but Abrazz will release them upon those who break our laws and his rules."

"I see. I swore not to break your laws," I reply as we walk back into the village again. Every one of the villagers stands in awe looking at us. He points towards the hut and we go inside. I turned around to ask the chief another question, but he had disappeared, leaving Kevin standing, looking at me.

"Where did you go Edward?"

"The chief took me to a plateau where their God, Abrazz, sits. I have no idea what all he was saying; his English is quite unique," I answer as several guards come in and pull us out into the main plaza of the village, spears pointing at us all. Fearfully I stand, not knowing what to do, as the chief came out of another hut and exclaimed:

"We have a man amongst us who has broken the rules… YOU!" He pointed at Kevin and I turned to look at him. He shrugs his shoulders as the chief walked over, angrily.

"You took a young woman outside the village last night. You must repay for your abomination of this girl! Four days you must spend in there… if you live, you may leave, but if you die… you belong to Abrazz!"

I stood still, staring at Kevin, unable to speak a single word. He knew how important this third visit was to keep a good relationship with the new chief. Almost fifteen years of respect down the drain.

"I'll do it, but you must let my friends leave!" Kevin finally responds.

The chief's anger shows as he answers viciously, "YOU DARE MAKE A DEMAND! No. They will stay just outside the village for these four days! GO… NOW!"

I watch as they grab Kevin and head into the forest, disappearing. I fear Kevin has doomed us all, as they push us just outside the circle of their village. All I can do is sit and wait to see the outcome of this act of betrayal. I watch well into the evening as they begin to dance around the fire that reaches towards the heavens. I have never seen this dance preformed before, and hope this isn't a curse on us.

When the fourth day arrives, and Kevin comes stumbling through the bush, bloodied and bitten by probably every bug known to us, the village is in an uproar of hate as they yell at him, angrily. The chief calms them down as he walks with Kevin towards me, stopping as Kevin falls to the ground in front of me.

Unhallowed

The chief looks at me harshly and speaks, "You must stay here for one more night. When the sun rises tomorrow, you are free to leave... but not before. And you will NEVER come back here again!"

"We will honor your request, and you have my word that we will never return here again," I reply, worried, as he glares.

"I know you will never return here, I don't need your word... I know you won't!"

He turns and shouts at the villagers who return his shouts. They drag Kevin back to our tent, and once alone I ask, "Why Kevin, why?"

"What harm did I do? She wanted to sleep with me, and she practically seduced me," he whispers back to me, clearly fatigued.

I watch as he goes limp, and Zima replies, "Don't worry, he is alive, just weak. Mr. Robinson, Sir... May I speak with you in private?"

"Of course, this way," I tell him, walking towards the little fire we have. He looks petrified as he barely manages to spit out a sentence, "We must leave here, NOW..."

"I gave my word; we must stay until tomorrow morning," I remind him, seeing him look towards the village.

"You don't understand, Mr. Robinson. By morning we may be...!"

"Zima, I am NOT going to dishonor my word!" I reply, watching him shake. He leans closer, earnestly.

"Mister Robinson… you DON'T understand. The dance they're doing isn't anything good! We must leave NOW!"

"Zima, ENOUGH! I gave my word, and a man is nothing without his word. Go see to Kevin and make sure he is alright," I answer firmly, pointing for him to go into the tent to tend to Kevin. He walks back into the tent, looking back only once at me.

That night, watching as they danced around the fire that raged on, I saw two of them holding what looked like the coffins from the willow tree we forbidden to look at. I watched on as they danced and passed the coffins between them, and after an hour a man and woman screamed. The fire turned blood red for a moment and then returned to a dull orange. Zima, coming up to me, commented on the scene, "Kevin is resting, but we are too late now Mr. Robinson… they have unleashed something evil!"

I looked at Zima, his own eyes looking at the ground while he spoke, and I asked, "What are you talking about, Zima? Every time we have come here they have always preformed their dances."

Looking like a ghost standing there, Zima explains, "Not this time Mr. Robinson. This is what I was trying to tell you before…" He grabs his throat, and pulls a spider off, throwing it to the ground. He gasps for breath as he falls to the ground and begins convulsing.

The chief comes over to the edge of the circle and looks at Zima, lying on the ground, dead. "It looks as if you have lost a member of your group… we will help you pack up in the morning."

Unhallowed

"Thank you" I respond, watching as he turns and walks away, confused by the turn of events.

Morning comes and, true to their word, the villagers help us leave. I look back one last time, to see them standing, glaring at us, as we leave for the last time.

Don. P. Pankratz

Strange things

Hailey and I are stuck in the mud. As I try to push the car, and Hailey gives it the gas, I have come to realize this is futile and the wheels are inevitably stuck. I walk around the car as she continues to gun the engine. With lightning flashing and thunder almost popping my eardrums, we decide to try to find a place out of the storm. After gathering a few items from the backseat, we walked down the road until, after about twenty minutes of slipping and sliding on this wretched dirt road, Hailey points out a little house with a flickering light inside. A glimmer of hope to get out of the rain. It looks like the house is about a quarter mile from the road, the light glimmering like a signal from the heavens. We slosh through the mud as we approach the door, and bang. No one answers, but the door opens.

Hailey breaks the silence: "Hello…? Is anyone here?"

We hear no answer, but walk in and look around. It appears as though the house I empty. Getting out of our wet clothes and hanging them on the old coat rack in the corner, we sit down in front of the fire to warm ourselves up. My arm around Hailey as we snuggle, I ask her, "Remember last year when I scored that touchdown and we won the 1952 high school championship game? I know you remember what we did afterwards."

Hailey looks at me smiling, as she replies, "Yes, I remember. You still have your hair slicked back and that pretty boy face that I love so much."

"What about you? You still have that golden blonde hair done up in a bun... you're still my cheerleader. That perfume you wear that drives me mad. Most of all, I still have you!" I reply as I lean in for a kiss.

I lean Hailey down and run my hand up her leg. As we make sweet passionate love by the fire, I can't help but feel like there is someone watching us.

Hailey stops me and asks, "Do you feel like we're being watched Tim?"

"Yeah, I do?" I reply, looking around the room. We sit there listening to the lightning and thunder crash outside as the floor creaks. Looking at Hailey, in just her bra and panties, I snuggle close, leaning in for another kiss, but Hailey pushes me away.

"Please not here. There is something creepy going on."

We hear another creak and frantically look around, waiting for someone to come out into the open, but no one does. The light flickers, sending shadows all around. It's just after midnight, and we lay down again. As I gently move my hand up her leg, causing her goosebumps, Hailey asserts:

"Will you quit that?"

Leaning in and kissing her shoulder, I cover her up with the musty old blanket lying beside the wood burning stove, and we try to get some sleep despite the crashing thunder making it impossible. Startled by a scratching noise, I jerk awake and look around for the source only to be startled by a young woman's image in a mirror hanging on the wall. She can't be more then maybe thirteen, and her mouth moves as if she is screaming at me, but I cannot hear a word she is saying. I just watch this young woman's brown hair and eyes. She is dressed in clothes from around the turn of the century and is anxiously pointing to the living room… towards Hailey. She eventually vanishes from the mirror, I shake my head, and look around again. The scratching stops.

(BANG)

Looking for what made the sound, I inch my way into the kitchen. Not seeing anything, I lay back down beside my Hailey, and she feels as cold as ice. I lay close to her, trying to warm her up, but only find myself becoming colder. Getting up again, I grab a couple more pieces of wood and place them on the fire, hoping to warm her up. I lay back down, and we both close our eyes.

As the light creeps in through the kitchen, signaling morning's arrival, the storm is still going strong. Getting up, I head to the kitchen and find an old coffee pot. I try the water pump but it just makes a squeaking noise. Walking out onto the front porch, I stick the empty pot into the storm and watch as the rain slowly fills the container. I find a couple old tea bags in the cupboard and sniff them to see if they are any good. Placing the coffee pot on top of the wood-burning stove to boil, I call to Hailey: "Hailey! Wake up…Hailey…?"

A whispered voice of a woman responds, "Tim… it's too late!"

Looking at Hailey still laying on the floor, I shout into the air: "What do you mean it's too late?" There is no response as I try waking her up, kneeling behind her, placing my hand in front of her. She is still. I Remove the blanket from over her face and realize that she is dead.

She has a look of fear on her face as if someone sucked her soul out of her body. Trying to figure out what happened to her, and what I am going to do, I gaze around in the grayish light of the room. There is no phone anywhere. I cover Hailey up, as I begin to sob, so I do not have to see the horrified look on her face anymore. My mind starts thinking back to the woman in the mirror, and I sit there, pondering what to do now with no way of getting help.

Standing up and walking around the house, I find an old desk and absent mindedly look at the book sitting open on top. Flipping back the fragile pages, my eyes scan the words on the first page:

"Sir Edwin Robinson;

October 1, 1895

We had great success on this expedition to the Spirit tribe of the rainforest near Africa. This being our second excursion here, the chief acknowledged our existence after we gave him a gold necklace. They allowed us to partake in their celebration of harvests, and we tried to accustom ourselves to their dance and offerings to their gods.

Watching as they beheaded a known thief for touching a sacred pendant attached to a skeleton hand, we were quite amazed at the accuracy of their killing methods. On our third night, my business partner Kelvin James, offered the chief a trade of goods. He was more than happy, exchanging two intact skulls for three bottles of whiskey. The skulls were tremendously intriguing; one had an interesting indent in the middle, between the eyes, and the other looks like they had no cheekbones. On the last day, the chief had a supper in our honor. Before our departure, he welcomed us back anytime.

Sir Edwin Robinson;

September 5, 1896

"Our fourth trip to the Spirit tribe of the rainforest wasn't a great success. Upon arrival, we learned the chief of the tribe had passed away just three months earlier. May God hold his soul sincerely. The new leader is NOT as welcoming as the previous. He treated us as if we were diseased and brought nothing of interest to him but bad luck. He made noteworthy mention of calling us demons of hell. They are allowing us to stay, however, just outside the village. We were instructed not to speak to anyone but the interpreter. On the third night of our stay they were holding various rituals, and at one point I swear they were calling out our names with the words "Dre" and "Succubus." The first night before we arrived, my business partner, Kelvin James, slept with a woman outside the village. Apparently she had provided us with some information on our last trip. From what I learned later, Kelvin said she wanted to sleep with him."

(Creak)

I look around to see if anyone is there but find the room around me still empty. After a few minutes, I return my gaze to the book and continue reading.

"The interpreter told me that Kelvin would have to endure the grave if he were guilty, and he would not return. The same day, Kelvin was exiled into the forest where he would have to survive, for four days and nights, by himself. If he survived, only the village, not the Gods, would curse him. The interpreter explained to me the curse meant that Kelvin would never have a relationship with a woman again. I tried to inquire further on that, but I got nothing in return. If Kelvin died during those four days that meant the gods took it upon themselves to cleanse him of his evil deeds. After four days, Kelvin did come back, torn up by the bushes and insects that roam these parts. We awakened the next morning with symbols painted on our chests and faces."

A whispered voice of a woman brought me back to reality again: "Leave before it comes for you too…"

Fearfully looking around, I still saw nothing, and continued reading.

"The symbols on our faces were triangles with lines transversely through them to the left. The one on my chest was a circle with a star in the middle and blood in the center. Neither of us understood why these were painted on our bodies. The interpreter tried to explain that they were the symbols for sending a demon to curse us. We didn't take it seriously, though. It just seemed like the tribe's way of scaring us away. The chief gave both Kelvin and me a carved horn to take back with us. We thankfully accepted the gifts in hopes we could return here again.

Sir Edwin Robinson

February 2, 1898,

After arriving home from our last trip to the jungle, my business partner fell ill with malaria. The doctors have been treating him with the best medicines, but it still up in the air if he will make a full recovery or not. Another member of our team, Jack Roslyn, died on the ship. He had strange markings on his body; A new disease perhaps, but it was a painful death as he suffered for 27 days before succumbing. The doctor aboard the ship had no idea what this disease was. We buried him, out at sea, immediately after his 'death' as not to contaminate the rest of the ship. From the harbor of Prince Edward Island to Saskatoon was quite a long journey, but I feel I should be home quickly. I have so many items to go through and catalog, but I cannot wait to see the look on my wife Margaret's face when she sees me again. At least this time this is my final expedition. I have enough items to keep me busy for the next sixty years. I hope she enjoys the gifts I have brought her as well.

February 4, 1898

Today was my second day at home. My wife, Margaret, enjoyed her gift of perfume, a necklace, and a ring. I have begun cataloging these items, but for some of them I cannot remember where they came from. I lost my notepad on the ship, and have tried, in vain, to get a telegraph out. I prayed to God I could find that notebook for without it I am just a blind mouse, looking for safety in a house of cats.

May 27, 1898

I still have not received word about my notepad. I have become very desperate in a manner of speaking. I can remember where certain items came from, but it will not be a complete collection if I do not have the correct information. I have received word that my partner Kelvin James has passed on in the most violent of ways. After winning his battle with malaria, his mental state went downhill from there. According to his wife Jeanine, he heard voices telling him to do things. She said they were driving him crazy. There were a vast number of mental changes since he returned home. She had mentioned that one night it was so hot in the house, which all the snow melted for about two feet around. He became violent on many occasions and then lastly, he took his own life. I can only hope whatever afflicted him does not afflict anyone else.

October 18, 1898

I have finally gotten word from the ship! They have found my notebook, and I should be receiving it in the next 20 days. This will give me a significant boost in my work; all I have been able to do is just study the pieces. I hope that this notepad arrives even sooner than expected. The museum has been on my tail about what I have, and I will be overjoyed when I can tell them what these pieces represent.

November 5, 1898

Finally, my notepad has arrived, and I have begun processing these precious items. I ran across a strange one, and I could not seem to find what it is. Either I have forgotten to write down this article, or someone just put this piece in with the others mistakenly. I have placed it aside on a shelf for the time being, as a reminder to look at the fanged creature later.

May 12, 1899,

I find the goings-on as of late particularly disturbing. My wife Margaret has fallen ill several times, and right before she fell ill she complained of being touched. She could not tell me by whom, but the strange voices I have heard as of late are exceedingly distressing. Two nights ago, I found myself awoken outside digging a trench in a circle. There was no reason for me to be out there digging. I fear that something beyond my comprehension is invading my body from within. I have chosen to keep working and have been using my faith in the Lord above to quench this thing. I fear I may have bought something from the twilight of the jungles home with me.

May 28, 1899,

Unhallowed

I know not what is going on within me. I drew blood from my wife today. I thought it was an accident, but she said I did it on purpose. I'm waiting for my business partner's wife to send me the items he was working on, but I just found out earlier this week she has passed as well in a most horrific way. She jumped from a Cliffside, with nothing left behind to offer an explanation. That was the most difficult death. I am starting to wonder if maybe on that last expedition my business partner did not thrust upon us an entity of sorts. I find the voices becoming clearer in their attempt to persuade me to do as they ask.

June 17, 1899,

I have done the unthinkable. Margaret has passed at my hands. I have buried her out by the old Willow tree. I have broken my heart with this act of maliciousness on my part. I could not deny it was me who perpetrated this as it was my hands around her neck. These voices are becoming stringently more intelligent. I fear I will live out my days, alone, in this home. As much as I have faith in the Lord above, I find myself walking through the coals of hell.

June 19, 1899,

I must be going crazy. I heard my wife has yelling at me for what I have done to her every day since her passing. I have apologized as many times as I prayed for forgiveness. I fear I have gone beyond insane at this moment. I woke up this morning and found scratches on my chest as if someone were trying to dig out my heart. I am finding it harder and harder to continue with my work. I came across an artifact I cannot explain or decipher. The amulet has a picture of a man and a bird of sorts surrounding him with his wings. I have no possible idea of what it represents, or where I found it.

July 28, 1899,

I have barricaded myself inside my room. Yesterday I went into town, picked up a harlot, and brought her back to my home. After an age of debauchery, I murdered her. My bed is stained with her blood, and I fear I can no longer be around people. These voices are becoming quite natural and controlling. I have buried her, next to my wife, by the Willow tree. I fear I will soon hear her voice calling me, too. My head is so overwhelmed with these sounds that I can no longer concentrate one moment on my gendered tasks. I keep the unknown amulet in front of me in hopes of deciphering its meaning.

August 2, 1899,

As I feared, the harlot has begun haunting me as well, like my wife. As much as I have fallen to my knees, and prayed for the Lord to guide me, I had all but failed in the attempt to reach him. Something has gotten into my room, or in my sleep…I don't know anymore… I have gone to my room. My door was ajar this morning, and looking out my window, I see that I have completed the circular trench. I have no idea what is happening within me. I can pray that if it is going to take my life, it takes me hastily.

September 23, 1899,

I have begged the Lord for the last time to help me. The trench outside now has a star in the middle of it. I know not of how they got there, but since it has been there I hear scratching on the walls. The sole way to describe the sound is a scratching like rusty nails across a chalkboard. A slate of memory has me thinking about what the interpreter had told us before leaving the village. I fear a demon of sorts is upon me. I sure hope it leaves soon, as I have little supplies in my room to hold out against it.

September 24, 1899,

I saw the devil last night. Right in front of my eyes, he dug up my wife, and the harlot, and proceeded to defile them in front of my window. I broke down as I saw my wife's face. A short time after he defiled them, they began walking around the house, asking me to let them inside my room. I refused to allow them inside, and the demon looked deep into my eyes. The look told me he was coming for me next. The voices in my head tormented me even worse than ever while the demon, my wife, and the harlot all made appearances in front of the window wanting me to let them inside. The saddened look on their faces was like God himself condemning me. I know not what I can do anymore; my strength becomes diminutive compared to the might of what awaits me outside.

September 26, 1899,

I have not any strength left to fight off this demon, nor my wife, or the harlot any longer. I fear this will be my last entry. The persistent scratching on the walls seems to be getting closer, and I sorely wish I knew what was going to happen to me. I only know that eventually …death… will be mine. I honestly regret everything I have done and can hope forgiveness is thrust upon me. I, Sir Edwin Robinson, can just hope that my death ends this demon."

I close the journal and get up, walking out of the room. Looking at the living room floor, where Hailey had been, she is now gone. "Hailey!" I shout. The storm still rages outside, and the doors open. Running towards the door, I try to find her, but she is gone. Footprints on the front porch are the only thing I see. Walking outside in an attempt to find her, I turn to go back inside and a black creature strikes my face. I fall to the ground, blood running down my face, and the creature steps on my head and shouts:

"You dare invade my home? You will suffer the same fate as your girlfriend."

Before I can say a word, everything goes black and silent.

Unhallowed

44 years later, Bedford Road Collegiate, May 12, 1996

Walking into the school, looking at everyone as I pass by, I smile at some, but am straight-faced with others. I'm headed down the hall towards class when I see Rick sitting on the bench. Walking up to him and nudging his shoulder, I ask, "Hey, are we still going to have a party this weekend?"

Rick looks at me, and he has that look that says "there ain't no party". He shakes his head and replies, "We can't have it at my place this weekend, Darren. My parents decided to stay home instead of going out like they regularly do. They suck."

"Well, maybe we can find someone else who has a place to party?" I reply.

"Yeah, maybe. I'll ask around at lunch and see if anyone knows of a location where we can have the party of the century."

"Right on Rick. I'll ask around, too. Maybe we can find someone who has a rocking place."

"I hope so. We have almost a truckload of beer and whiskey, and I want to get laid this weekend."

"Ah, that would be so awesome. Two girls in bed with me doing everything I want. Yeah that would be just right on." I reply as a girl walks by and Rick watches her for a moment before replying.

"I would just be happy if Pamela noticed me. I'd tap her as quick as could be."

"You've had a thing for Pamela for a while now, haven't you?" I respond, making the boner motion with my arm.

Rick cracks a bit of a smile and replies, "Yeah. Three years now, but Pamela has never said more than 'hi'."

"Well, if we have this party she'll have no choice but to notice you, and appreciate everything you could do for her," I reply, nodding my head as Rick contemplates for a moment. He nods his head and replies, "Yeah, that would definitely bring up my game some."

This guy built like a steam engine stops walking and stands in front of us, and asks, "Did I hear you guys right? You guys want to throw a party this weekend?"

"Yeah, you heard right. Who the hell are you anyway?" I reply looking him up and down, suspiciously.

"The name's Scott. I'm new to the school."

Rick's eyes open wide. "Holy shit. You're the troublemaker, aren't you?"

Scott looks at Rick and leans towards him stating. "No, I'm not the troublemaker. I just don't back down when shit comes my way."

"Yeah on the first day you were here you beat up all those jocks." I reply laughing.

"I basically beat them up, because they were too damn stupid to back off."

"Yeah well, they sure stay away from you now." I reply, still laughing harder than ever.

"That's why I say I'm not a troublemaker; they learned their lesson the hard way. Anyway, a friend of mine knows of an abandoned place where we could hold the party…if you guys still want to party?"

"Oh, we always want to party, man. Just finding places to have the party has been difficult these last few weeks."

Rick looks up at Scott and finally speaks, "I'm Rick, by the way. And this is Darren. An abandoned place, hey? How empty is this place?"

Scott leans even closer and replies, "This place is so abandoned that nobody's lived there for like 70 years. The house is still standing. Maybe not rock solid, but it would be out of the way of any cops or parents showing up."

Rick smiles and responds, "Nice. Can you set this up?"

Scott nods, "Yeah I'll talk to my friend this evening, I'll go take a look at it, and see what's in need of repair."

"Sweet. If you can do that, we'll get everyone invited." I state, smiling ear to ear.

"You got it. Talk to you guys later."

Watching as Scott walks away, I note that he's built like a cast-iron engine. Those poor jocks never stood a chance. He had them all crying like babies by the end of it.

"So, do you think he'll come through?" I ask Rick.

"I think so, Darren. He doesn't seem like the type to bullshit about something like that."

"Cool. I cannot wait to start inviting girls to this party. We are going to get so many numbers; we'll feel like Hugh Hefner."

Rick laughs and responds. "You better quit thinking like that, or you'll blow your top before we get to class."

"Yeah, maybe you're right Rick." I reply, still laughing.

After school, we see Scott in the parking lot. Walking over to him by his truck, Scott notices us, and shouts:

"Hey guys, what's up? I talked to my friend, he said we're good to go. I'm going to head there tonight and check it out."

"That's great... umm? We're just wondering if we could tag along with you, and see the place?"

Scott throws his books in the back of his truck and replies, "Sure, no problem. Rhe more help I can get, the faster we can fix her up. I'll be heading there in a while, I just got to pick up a few planks of lumber before we go."

"We're just curious about what this place looks like."

Hopping in his truck, Scott turns to reply, "Like I said nobody's lived there for about 70 years, so I'm sure that sounds like a rat's fucking nest."

"Yeah, I bet it does. But we'll get it all spiffed up."

We pile into Scott's truck, and he takes off to the lumberyard. He picks up four sheets of plywood and a dozen two by fours. We head west out of town and drive for about 20 minutes before Scott turns onto a back road. As the truck jumps and bounces all over the place, Rick shouts:

"Holy cow is this way bumpy."

Scott holds onto the steering wheel for dear life as he replies, "Yeah, good old Saskatchewan backroads."

Rick hits the roof of the truck as he tries talking, "So how far is it from here?"

"It should just be past the next hill"

The greenish brown fields zip by the roadside, and I can't help but note, "Wow, there is nothing around here, except for wheat fields."

Scott smiles as he bounces around and explains, "That's what makes it a great party spot. Nobody ever comes down these roads, except for the farmers who live around here, and they are far and few between. There's the house right there, off to the right."

"Wow. It definitely looks like it's been deserted for a while. Hopefully you have got some tools to cut down some of those weeds."

"Yes, I got a little handheld swath to chop down some of that shit. If you guys start cutting down the plants, I'll start fixing the house up a bit."

We pull up in front of the house and stop. We pause a moment, looking at the creepy one story broken down house surrounded by weeds six-feet high before getting out. Walking through the house, a musty old smell lingers in the air and the floor creaks with every step as we move from room to room.

Rick pops up and shouts, "Holy... this place has literally NOTHING!"

"Damn. I haven't seen a wood burning stove in years. Look, there's even a blanket on the floor. What a great place to get laid," I reply.

"Come on Darren. Get your head out of your fucking ass for a while. Let's just worry about getting this place fixed up so we can have the party tomorrow night."

"Okay, Rick. This house smells so bad," I respond, covering my nose.

Scott opens the one door and shouts out, "Hey! Look at this you guys! This old desk has got to be at least 100 years old."

"Holy shit yeah. Someone even left a book behind. I'm going to take a look at it before we start."

Scott calls out a warning as he watches me go inside the room: "Go ahead. Just watch for the floor though. You never know when one of those boards is going to give out."

"Hey Scott? Rick? The name on this book is Sir Edwin Robinson. Can you imagine having a name like that, what a joke?" I laugh.

Rick also chuckles, "Yeah, no kidding. I dub thee, Sir Darren of Dick wad."

Scott bangs on the wall a he laughs, dust falling with every hit. Becoming serious, he responds, "Ha-ha-ha. Good one guys. Now let's get this place fixed up."

We make our way out of the room and Scott starts putting the two by fours on the porch while Rick and I start picking the weeds around the house. Two hours go bybefore we stop for a break.

Looking at the patched porch, Rick says, "Damn Scott. You've got carpentry down to a science, don't you?"

"Yes, I do. I've been working construction for the last year. This house is in fact not that bad; most of the work needed is just superficial."

"Yeah, I just never thought I'd see the day where a weed was taller than me. Holy shit, are they tall. It's almost like cutting down a damn tree." I reply, laughing, as Scott replies:

"Well just think about it. Another few hours and you should have the rest of those cut down."

"I sure hope so," Rick responds, "at least most of the weeds will hide the party."

Scott points out the weeds are still pretty close to the house and states, "Yeah, just make sure you make enough room for a bonfire as well. If you leave too many weeds up, and too close to the fire, and we won't be going anywhere until after we're fried."

Rick shakes his head as he grabs the swath, "I'll make sure, I cut far enough out."

We get back to work chopping the weeds down, while Scott continues to repairt the house. While swathing the weeds down behind the house, I come across a metallic object laying by a well that looks like a rusty amulet. I pick it up but don't think much of it as I throw the amulet further into the weeds. After another hour of hacking at weeds, Rick makes a noise as he trips in a hole in the ground.

"You alright man?" I shout.

Rick sits on the ground holding his ankle and answers, "My ankle hurts pretty bad, but I'll be fine."

Scott, coming around the house, shouts at us, "What the hell's going on back there? I don't hear no chopping!"

"Rick fell into a kind of trench," I reply as Scott comes and kneels down to look at Rick's ankle.

Confused, Scott replies, "A trench? There shouldn't be a trench there. Let me see it."

I pick up the swath and start cutting away, exposing a circular shaped trench with what looks like a star in the middle. Scott stands up and stares in awe, thinking out loud, "What the hell is this?"

"Holy shit. It looks like Satanists were here at one time. That's definitely a pentagram."

"What the hell's a pentagram doing here?" I ask as Scott, who stands next to me, snickering.

"Chances are, they were just like you guys: out looking for a place to summon Satan. I wouldn't worry about it. It's actually a great place to have a bonfire. The trench there will keep the fire inside and stop it from spreading."

Rick, still sitting on the ground and rubbing at his ankle, responds, "Yeah, I guess?"

Scott looks at us both again, "Nice, there's just one last thing we have to do. You going to be alright, Rick?"

"Yeah I'll be all right; I'll just wrap my shirt around it."

We head back over to our tools and continue swathing, cutting a good twenty-feet away from the trench. After a while I hit a log and decide to stop cutting and instead start clearing up the area. Throwing the chopped weeds over by the old well behind the house, I glance into the well, seeing the old stones layered and cracked. I spit and listen to hear the sound of it hitting the water, but nothing comes back. Shrugging my shoulders as I grab another batch of weeds and carry them to the well, a pungent smell wafts past me, causing me to gag. I look around to see where the smell could be originating from. As I walk past the well and into the field, slowly the smell becomes more discernable and the swarming flies make it hard to see. Suddenly I hear Scott shouting, "DARREN!"

"I'LL BE RIGHT THERE!" I yell back, swatting my hand back and forth trying to clear the flies away. I stumble, tripping over something, and find myself looking into the face of an almost decomposed animal. Throwing up on it, I try pushing up but my hand slips. I stare in horror at this thing as a snake crawls out of its eye socket. Getting up this time, staring around and still swatting the flies, I shout to the others, "Holy shit! SCOTT, RICK… COME HERE!"

I can't stop staring at the mound of dead animals, decomposing, and the stench is overpowering, as Scott comes around the house.

"Jesus Christ! What the hell man? What is that tortuous smell?"

"You think that's torturous, try slipping in this shit!" I reply, wiping my arms off.

Scott looks around at the corpses and responds, "I think you better change before getting back in my truck. I have some extra water you can use to clean up."

"Thanks, I don't even want to be around myself… you don't think this will ruin our party, do you?" I ask.

"This would ruin anything, period! I wonder though, what the hell killed all these animals and just left them here?"

Pulling a piece of rotting flesh off my shirt, I respond. "I don't know, but that one looks as if something took a bite out of its skull."

"Shit. I've never seen teeth marks like that before, have you?"

Taking a closer look, I answer, "it looks like piranha teeth to me, but that's impossible.

"Yeah… they do, don't they? Huh. Maybe if we cover these things up it will mask the smell a bit?"

"Probably. I'm looking to have a good time, and that includes puking over a toilet, but I'd prefer it to be because I'm drunk." I reply, making Scott laugh.

"I hear you. I'll go let Rick know and we'll grab a couple of shovels."

"Okay…." I answer, still fixated on the corpses. Once I can no longer hear Scott's footsteps, an uneasy feeling of despair washes over me. Glancing around, I swear I see a girl run past whispering, "Get out of here!"

The feeling quickly passes, and Scott comes back, passing me a shovel. After couple of hours shoveling dirt, darkness approaches and the mound of corpses is somewhat buried. We pack up our belongings into Scott's truck, and head for home.

Party time!

The next day we use the school printer to make copies of the flyers announcing the party, and the directions to get there. Darren and I hand them out at break, lunch and, after school. It's only after all of the flyers are gone that I realize I put the wrong date on them. "Shit. How the hell did we fuck up on the date?"

Darren shakes his head in disbelief as he replies. "I don't know man, but I guess we're having the party tomorrow night."

"Yeah, I guess. Mind you, we could always start the party a day early," I reply while I pat Darren on the shoulder.

"What do you mean Rick?"

"I mean we can get some of our friends together and we can start the party a day early. That way, when the rest of the partygoers come we'll already be toasted, so to speak."

"That's not a bad idea, Rick. We did put bring your own alcohol, so our drinking is not going to affect the amount we have. Yeah, let's do it."

"Great, I'll talk to some people in my class and you talk to some of the ones in yours, and we'll see if we can get a little pre-party going." I exclaim as we walk down the hall together.

After talking to a few people, and spreading the word about the get-together tonight, the bell rings and I can finally get out of school. Darren and Scott meet me at my place and we load up Scott's truck, taking two trips to get all the alcohol to our party palace.

By the time we arrive with the second load, there are already 3 cars parked and 12 people standing outside, waiting for us. Getting out of the truck to greet people, I don't see Patricia anywhere. We launch the bonfire, and it soon engulfs the entire trench in a twenty-foot high flame.

"Woah!" I shout, and everyone shares my amazement at how fast the fire ignites. I walk up to a girl I don't recognize and introduce myself: "Hi, my name's Rick. What's yours?"

She turns to look at me, and replies, "Janice."

"So, are you here alone tonight?" I ask excitedly, as she looks at me strange and coldly responds.

"Yeah... but you have another thing coming if you think I'm going to be with you. You don't think everyone here knows how you treat Darren, but we do."

"We're just messing around." I state, watching her flip me off and walk to the other side of the fire. Walking around with a beer in hand, I see Brenda sitting on a lawn chair listening to Skid Row's "18 and life". Watching as she bobs to the tune, I smile as I imagine other ideas for her. "Hi. Brenda," I break the silence, standing beside her.

She glances at me and responds. "This is a sweet spot you got here. You can even see the stars."

"Oh, well yeah. I never even noticed that. Yeah, the stars sure are twinkling bright tonight." I check her out, and she smiles uncomfortably, looking back up at the stars.

"I love looking up at the stars at night. There's just something about them that makes you feel calm all over."

"Oh yes, I can see what you mean. Are you here all alone?" I ask inquisitively, still looking up at the stars.

She looks back at me, and her eyes lose their twinkle as she replies, "No, I'm here with a couple of friends."

"Hopefully one of them isn't a boyfriend?" I reply, smiling.

"No. He didn't want to come, so I came without him."

"Darn. I was hoping you weren't snatched up. I would love to go out with you."

"Yeah, that's a real shame. I'll let Bobby know you were interested in me, though."

"No, there's no need to let anyone know." I hurriedly answer, looking around nervously. I turn away from her as she mumbles something under her breath. Walking around again, I see someone in the twilight just outside the brightness of the fire. Walking over to her, I sit down beside a girl I've never seen before. Sliding a little closer, I ask, "How's it going back here?"

She turns towards me, and responds, "Better, now that you are here. Is this your party?"

"Yes, mine and Darren's party!" I respond, seeing a smile emerge on her face as she scoots a little closer. "I'm glad to be back here, with you. What's your name?"

She smiles, the light of the fire barely kissing her face, as she softly replies, "Margaret. This is one sweet party you have here, I can't wait to see what happens when you all let loose."

"Margaret's a sexy name. Yeah, our parties usually have a triple xxx rating!" I place my hand on her leg, and her eyes lock onto my mine as she touches my thigh.

"Is it a sexy name? Then why haven't I been touched in so long? X-rated, huh? A young man like you should be able to make a new woman of me then."

"Well that's a shame, Margaret, because you're gorgeous. If I were going out with you I'd be all over you," I exclaim, barely able to contain my enthusiasm. She leans in even closer, and I feel her breath on my neck as she places her mouth near my ear and whispers.

"Really? I would like that actually. What would you do to me?"

"Oh… first, I would kiss you all over; there would not be a spot where my hands would not touch you."

She smiles as my hand moves up to her hip. Her hand meets mine as she continues, "Oh, that sounds like something I would like. Having your hands all over me is making me hot. Why don't we go back here, so I can do things to you that you will never forget?"

Sliding her mouth towards mine and running her tongue across my lips, we kiss for a while. Pulling back as her hand crawls up my leg and touches my enthusiasm.

"Alright. You lead the way, Margaret."

Getting up, my hand slips to her butt as I squeeze, and she smiles. We walk for a bit, holding hands as we trample through the thick weeds until Margaret stops, and turns to me.

"This looks like a good spot; don't you think so Rick?"

"Any place you pick would be perfect," I respond, sliding my hand up her sides as she begins undressing quickly. She grabs my shirt and tears it away like a tiger. Running my hands up and down her sides, she makes the sweetest moans. Sitting her down, leaning up against this old willow tree, we start making out nonchalantly at first and then passionately.

Before long I'm on top of her while she whispers in my ear. "Oh Rick. I want you inside me. I want you to fill me, with your love."

"I want you so bad," I reply, moaning as every little touch drives me to ecstasy while touching and kissing her.

As I begin to thrust, a weird feeling comes over me; a feeling I do not understand. It feels as though something is crawling all over me. I stop, asking, "Margaret, do you feel… like ants are crawling all over you?"

"No Rick, all I feel is you. Now give it to me before I explode."

As we get heavier into it, the feeling becomes more and more noticeable. It feels like a million ants crawling are all over me, and before long, it becomes a constant itch.

I ask again, "Are you sure you don't feel anything, Margaret? I just have this creepy feeling, all over."

She moans as she replies, "I don't feel anything but you Rick. Don't worry about anything except for finishing what you started."

Looking at her shadow, I reply, "I can't hold it anymore, I'm coming."

A few moments after finishing, the feeling is still driving me nuts, but Margaret excitedly states, "Oh, Rick. Let's go again."

"Okay, you're going to have to give me a few minutes though." I respond, still huffing.

Getting up, I still have that feeling. I wipe where it feels like things are crawling over me and feel something slimy. I search around for my pants, finally finding my lighter. Flicking it, as the flame dances around, I run it over my arm to see a few maggots crawling on me. I begin batting them off quickly.

"Hey, Margaret! I think we must be close to a dead animal; I have maggots crawling over me."

"Come on Rick, let's do it again; don't let a few worms ruin the mood. Don't you want me again?"

I drop to my knees, flicking the lighter again, and bring the lighter's flame closer to Margaret's face. As the light dances across, her face looks as if she's been dead for years.

I audibly gasp, dropping the lighter. "Oh dear God, what happened to your face?"

She smiles, maggots falling from her mouth, and leans towards me saying, "Nothing babe. Come here."

Before I can say, or do anything, she grabs me and brings me down to the ground, holding me tight against her. Placing her mouth over mine, any sounds I make are muffled. I try fighting her off, but it is no use. The maggots crawl in my mouth as I continue to fight, and I feel a cold hand reach for my arm. Suddenly, another woman's soft voice cuts through.

"Well, it looks like someone's having fun without me! I'll join you two."

Margaret pushes my face down to her breasts as she replies to this new voice, "Oh, yes. Join us, Hailey. Rick did you hear that? You'll get twice the pleasure now."

"HELP!" I scream, but my voice is muffled by Margaret's breast.

The other woman leans close and whispers in my ear, "Oh Rick, I'll make sure you never forget me. I am going to make your dreams come true."

Digging her nails into my back, I try desperately to scream for help. I feel teeth scraping along my back, pulling skin off.

I keep trying to get away, but Margaret bites my ear and whispers, "Do you like this, Rick? Two girls? I bet you never thought you would ever be in this situation. Don't worry, we know what we're doing."

Hailey's hand reaches down between my legs, and she runs her nails across me. I try to squirm free, but Margaret is holding me so tight I can barely breathe.

Hailey sits beside us and whispers into my other ear, "Rick, come on. If you aren't going to be humping Margaret, I am just going to have to assume you don't like women. Tell me that's not true."

Trying to punch Margaret, as I fight to escape her grasp, she whispers into my ear, "Yes, come on Rick. Where's the enthusiasm you had the first time?"

Margaret holds me even tighter, as the other woman's hand makes its way between my legs again.

"If you don't want love, perhaps I have a better idea for you."

I feel a sharp pain as she squeezes, not stopping until the pain is unbearable and I manage to shout, "It hurts, stop it!"

Margaret pulls me into her shoulder, and Hailey pulls so hard I almost pass out. Hailey laughs as she replies, "Well, Rick, I guess you don't like us, but you also no longer have your manhood."

Margaret holds me even tighter. "Too bad, I was really starting to like you; I guess you can go…"

Hailey holds tight onto me, as Margaret takes a bite into my cheek and Hailey bites my ribs. As I scream out, everything goes blank.

A taste of love

Walking around the fire, the flames swaying to the music playing as if it were alive, I smile at everyone as I pass by. Most people return the smiles. After making my way around the fire, I come to a stop and look around. "Has anyone seen Rick around?" I ask, curiously, as a woman answers me:

"The last I saw Rick, he was sitting over there with a girl. I think he was trying to get laid."

A burst of laughter crosses the calm night air. "Yes, that would be like him, thanks, everyone." I respond, as I walk over to where she was pointing. I turn back towards the front of the house to where Patricia and some of the girls are standing.

"Sorry, Patricia. I thought he genuinely liked you; I guess I was wrong." I reply, straight –faced.

Patricia looks and smiles at me as she looks at Scott and explains, "That's fine, I liked someone else anyway."

"Yeah, I figured you did. As hard as Rick tried to get your attention, if you wanted him you would have noticed. Who do you like anyway?" I ask, watching her look over at Scott again.

"I like Scott. He's a good guy. I heard his last girlfriend cheated on him; I would never do that to him."

"Does Scott know you like him?" I ask while Patricia stares at him, nervously. She shakes her head no.

Watching her blush as she turns to look at the ground, I encourage her, "Just go over there and talk to him. I know he is a decent person; he is the one that fixed up this place so we could have a party here. Just go over and let him know how you feel."

She looks at me and I nod. She stands there thoughtfully for a moment before replying, "Yeah, maybe you're right. Perhaps I will go over and speak to Scott. Thanks, Darren."

"You're welcome."

As she walks away slowly, as if she's trying to find some words to say before she gets to Scott, I mutter under my breath, "that's for your comment, Rick. Maybe next time, you'll think before saying something like that about me again."

Walking around some more, I grab another beer and open it up, taking a drink. Looking over at Scott and Patricia, talking and laughing together, I head into the house. I soon realize there is no bathroom to be found and walk back outside. I see a girl, standing by one of the cars, her long brown hair so curly and full of life. I walk over to where she is, and as I come closer she turns her head.

Cindy smiles at me, "Hey, Darren! How's it going?"

"Oh it's going alright, Cindy. How about yourself? Are you having fun?"

"Yeah. Not as much as I thought I'd be having; I thought more of my friends would be coming, but I guess they had better things to do tonight."

"Yeah, that's a shame. The party should be rocking tomorrow, though. That was our screw up; Rick misprinted the flyers to say the party is tomorrow." I reply, taking a drink.

"Yeah, I know. Rick was saying that you messed up on them."

Nodding my head. "He always blames me for his mistakes."

"Yeah, I noticed that. Why do you even hang around that guy?"

"I've known him since we were kids. I guess I just put up with him doing that kind of stuff because we're friends. Maybe my brains fell out of my back end, who knows." I reply, laughing, as Cindy giggles.

"You're funny, Darren."

"Thanks Cindy. I try to be. I'm sorry to hear about your boyfriend. That was a dog move if I ever saw one."

"Yeah, no kidding. I don't know how long he figured he was going to get away with dating three girls at one time. I was honestly just glad to find out before we had done anything."

Looking at her, her hair slightly covering her face in the light breeze, Cindy's eyes mirror the bon fire in the distance, making her more adorable.

"You deserve a guy who's going to be there for you," I answer, grinning as Cindy looks into her drink.

As her eyes slowly work their way up to mine, she responds, "True, but guys like that are harder to come by than you think."

"I know I have wanted to ask you out myself, but I just haven't had the nerve to say anything to you until now. Maybe it's the drink helping me along?" I look into her eyes as she grins at me.

"Really? I thought you didn't like me; every time I come around you you're always going the other way or hiding."

"I'm sorry. I do like you, and I like you a lot. I just did that because I didn't want you to see me turn as red as a lollipop. Besides, if you said no, Rick would have used that against me so many times."

"Well, Rick's not around right now, is he? You never know what would happen if you asked me now."

"That's right. ...Whew... Cindy, would you...like to go out with me sometime on a date?" I ask, feeling as if I am on fire from the inside.

Cindy's grin widens as she replies, "Well Darren, I don't really think that... I'm just kidding; yeah, I'll go out with you sometime... what about now? There's no better time than the present."

Taken aback as I look at her smiling, I lean in to kiss her cheek and the smell of cherries comes from her locket.

"Awesome! I promise I will not do anything like that other guy did. I'll make sure you are my number one."

Cindy looks at me, puts her arm on my shoulder and replies. "Darren. Don't worry about saying anything; let's just have fun, okay?"

"Okay, sorry, I am just excited."

"I know, I can see it in your eyes."

"Yes, but that's only because I am caught in the gaze of your brown eyes. I still can't believe we are going out."

Cindy laughs and responds, "Yeah, keep the corny mush at home."

I look into her eyes and see she's on the brink of laughter. "You had me going for a moment."

As I move my thumb across the top of her hand, Cindy smiles and responds, "Yeah, just be yourself. That's what I like about you; you don't have to try and impress me."

"Sorry, I guess I see Rick in everything I do. I will try and remove him from these thoughts."

"He really has been a pain for a long time, hasn't he?"

"Yeah I guess he has been. I didn't think it bothered me this much," I reply, lowering my head.

Cindy places her hand under my chin and lifts my head up, stating, "Don't worry, things are going to change. Once he sees you have a girlfriend, he will disappear. Once he can't push you around like he has been you'll come into your own. Friends don't treat each other the way he treats you."

"Now I wish I had asked you out last year when I first saw you. I was stupid not too," I reply, shaking my head.

"You wouldn't have liked me then, I was mad because I didn't want to come to this school. Now is a perfect time. Why don't you show me around this place?"

"Sure." I answer, taking her hand in mine. We slowly walk, snuggled up against each other, laughing; her hair smells like strawberries. I move my hand and slide it around her waist as we stop near the front of the house. Slowly moving around to her front, I lean in for a kiss. Our lips touch and an overwhelming feeling weakens my knees. Wrapping my arms around her, I slide my hand up into her hair as our passions unleash into bliss. I open my eyes, so I can see her beauty, and as her eyes open I see a glimmer that makes me want her even more.

Travis, passing by, stops and looks at us. "Darn, you two are together now?"

Cindy smiles and replies, "Yep… he's all mine!"

"She's all mine Travis, and I couldn't be happier," I answer, holding Cindy closer.

"That's awesome, you two. Darren, make sure to stay away from Rick. He'll kill this relationship quick."

Before I have a chance to say anything, Cindy jumps in, "Don't worry Travis; I'll set Rick straight if he tries to pull anything."

"Nobody is going to come between us, not without a fight anyways," I add, looking into Cindy's eyes.

Travis nods and replies, "Right-on! Have fun you two."

Cindy grabs me and states, "Don't worry, I plan too!"

As I watch Travis walk away, I turn my full attention to Cindy as I lean in and kiss her, slipping into bliss.

A broken moment

Seeing a couple kissing passionately, not wanting to bother them, I continue along until I see a man standing by a truck. As I get closer, recognizing Scott, I ask, "Hey, dude. Where's the bathroom?"

"Oh hey, Trevor. The bathroom's wherever a dark spot is; there's no working toilet here."

"Thanks, Scott." I answer, quickly. Seeing another couple of cars pulling into the driveway, I walk around to the back of the house, finding a nice little spot to take a leak. I unzip my pants and start to piss. After finishing, I hear a woman's inaudible whispers.

"What?" I ask, listening again.

"Let me help you with that."

Looking around, trying to see any movement, I call out, "Who are you? Where are you...? I can't see you?" I continue looking around at the darkness of the shadows.

"I'm down here."

Turning to the left, I get on all fours and start crawling around, trying to find her. Feeling around for a sign of this woman, I touch some skin.

"Is this you?" I ask, inquisitively, feeling something wet and warm.

She replies softly, "Yes, that's me. What strong hands you have. You must work out."

"Yes, I work out every other day."

"Oh, I like that. I know another muscle we can work out together... if you're interested?"

"I like the sound of that myself. What's your name?" I ask, feeling extremely happy inside. She whispers, "Sandra. I have a place we can go where we won't be disturbed."

Getting up, off my hands and knees, Sandra grabs my hand and we walk just outside the glow of the fire. A stench of something awful stings my nose as I ask, "Jesus... what is that?"

Sandra giggles as she responds, "It's the food of the Gods!"

"Dam... if that's what Gods eat, I'm not interested," I answer covering my nose. We continue walking and I can see the flickering light of the bonfire in the distance. We come to what looks like a tree in the shadows, and she falls to the ground, laughing.

"What's so funny?" I ask, confused.

Still laughing, she exclaims, "This is the craziest thing I have done in a long time. I haven't been so excited in years."

"What? Are you saying you haven't done it in a while?" I ask as she leans in and moans.

"That's precisely what I'm saying. It's been so lonely here; I'm looking for some company."

"Well, I think I can help you in that department, Sandra. I use it all the time." I laughingly answer as I undo my jeans.

Sandra replies. "Well, if you use it all the time, how come you're not down here with me?"

"Oh, don't worry. I'll be down there soon enough, and I'll be banging on your door." I respond as my jeans fall down to my ankles.

Dropping to the ground, my pants around my knees as I slide up to Sandra, I go to pull her panties down but she isn't wearing any. I position myself and begin. After a few minutes, it feels as though something is oozing all over me, and a godawful smell of something that has died emanates around me. I cannot stand it anymore and stop, sitting up.

"What the hell is that smell, and what's this thick slimly stuff all over me. 'Christ!'" I shout as I fling my hand around. Sandra replies.

"What's wrong baby? Don't you like women?"

"I do, but this feels like there something dripping all over me!" I exclaim.

"Oh, don't worry baby. You've just got me all wet."

"That's not what I am talking about; whatever this smell is, it's coming from you. What's coming from above stinks like piss and is disgusting too." I exclaim.

A dark eerie voice laughingly states, "Oh, I'm sorry, that must be me pissing on you."

Looking up and seeing a shadowy creature up on a tree limb, I shout, "Get down here and I'll kick your ass you stupid...."

"If that's what you want, then that's what you'll get."

Just at that moment, Sandra grabbed my arms and pulled me into her; I hear a thump on the ground, and he growls as his footsteps come closer. I try to pull away from Sandra, but it is useless; she has the strength of ten men. She grabs hold of my face and pulls me into her chest, and I have a rotten taste in my mouth. I throw up, but it has nowhere to go. I feel a hand on my groin, and hear the man laughing.

"What's this little thing here?"

I feel an extremely intense pain in my groin, and I try to yell, but the vomit in my mouth is stopping me. As Sandra holds tight, the creature laughs again.

"Now who's going to get their ass kicked? I guess you will want your penis back; here you go, right in your backside. Now, tell me...how does it feel, getting fucked up, Trevor? What, something in your mouth? You're so deprived of sex you cannot stop to talk to me? Oh, well if anyone asks you remember it was Dre who fucked you up."

The last thing I feel is a sharp pain in my ass as everything goes black

Loving every moment

Standing on the porch kissing, I pull. Back slowly and look into Cindy's eyes.

"I can't believe this is happening. Us together... I never want this to end."

"I hope this lasts a lifetime. I have a good feeling about you, Darren."

We walk into the house to be alone for a while; Cindy holds my hand as she leads me inside. We walk around, holding hands and leaning against one another, laughing. We saunter into a room; the one with the desk, and Cindy notices the book.

"Wow. This office is old. By the looks of that book it's about the same age as the bureau. Can I take a look at the book, Darren?"

"By all means, Cindy, be my guest," I reply, watching Cindy opening up the book.

After reading for a while, Cindy looks up at me and responds, "Man this Sir Edwin Robinson was having a rough time of it. I've heard of demons summoned to harass people, but not many that kill people. This individual one murdered his wife and the hooker. Sounds like he brought it on himself, though."

Watching the look of concern on Cindy's face, I respond, "Yeah, no kidding. What else does it say about him?" I ask, nervously watching as she continues to read the journal.

"Looks like there are more entries in here. There's a couple of blank pages and then it starts again."

Watching as she flips through the pages slowly, I ask again, "Don't leave me hanging here, what does it say?"

"Okay, just hold on. September 28, 1899: I have been without food for nearly four days now. The demon has made it known that it wants me. My thoughts turn sour every time I see this beast at the window. I had gotten a glimpse into its mind when we had those painted symbols on our bodies; it went straight through to my soul, apparently marking us. After my business partner had partaken in debauchery with that village girl, they sent this demon to rectify his wrongdoing. I will not be able to make that journey, to their community, and apologize for what he had done. I still do not know the name of the demon meant to take my life as of yet, and I fear there is more than one demon here. They seem to be by the old willow tree and only come out to mock my existence. My head hurts so much from the lack of food and drink. I fear before the day is through I will be no more than their plaything. I have attempted to give them back the amulet, but they just look at it and mock me again. I am at a loss for understanding how to get rid of something I know nothing about. The harlot is possessed no doubt; she always flaunts her wares nearby. I fear my thoughts are going to betray my body soon."

Looking at Cindy, concerned, I ask, "What's wrong Cindy?"

She stares confused out the window for a moment. She looks at the book and then me and states, "I wonder if he means that old tree I saw when we got here?"

"Yes, I believe there was a tree there. See? You can barely make it out by the light of the flames," I respond, pointing out the window. Cindy looks out the window and nods, as she begins reading once again:

"September 29, 1899: I am afraid this is the end for me; I have heard the demons walking around in the living area. The constant knocks on the door, and the whispers telling me they will spare my life if I open the door for them are constant. I have visions of a hellish fate which awaits me. The demon talks to me and tells me he will never leave this place until the virtue of that girl's honor is restored. The devil also mentioned that this ground would be unhallowed for all time. I have yet to know the name of my tormentor.

I have realized that I am in a wild state; trying to make out what is fact or fiction is one of the hardest tasks as of yet. I have watched many people hanging from that willow tree, and I must concur that this is not real. As much as I feel it is fiction, it still breaks my heart knowing those people were once my friends. Another demon has just come to the door of my room. This one says I will never rest in peace as long as my bones exist. During the rains last night, I managed to get two glasses of water from what dripped through the ceiling. My wife is still calling my name, and how I do want to run out and hold her close. I yell out to her that I am sorry, but she does not reply."

Cindy looks at me, as she eyes the room, and I see her shiver a little as if she senses something near.

"What's wrong, Cindy?" I ask, nervously looking around the room myself.

Cindy is still shaking a little as she replies, "I don't know, Darren... I feel as if there is something, or someone, in here with us."

She looks around for a few minutes and continues reading aloud:

"September 30, 1899: What a hellish night it has been. The demon has shown me the darkness where I will soon be. This place is such that... no human should ever be. I cannot foresee a way of stopping this demon and sending it back to where it came from. As the door to my room rattles more and more from the banging and scratching, I can only hope that once this demon has my soul that he will go back to where he once came..."

Cindy flips through the remaining pages quickly and states, "That's all there is. All the other pages are empty."

Looking at her worried, I blurt out, "You don't believe there was a demon here, do you?"

Cindy shakes her head slightly and replies, "I don't know, Darren. I know some of my friends think that demons do exist in our world."

"Really? Are any of your friends here tonight?" I ask, inquisitively looking rapidly around the room.

"One of them is," She replies, tapping on the window. Brenda and a few others look over. Cindy gestures for them to come in.

The silence in the room is cut suddenly by Scott, "Hey guys, what are you doing in here?"

Almost jumping out of my skin, I hurriedly reply, "Oh, hi Scott. Hi, Patricia. Cindy was just reading from that book on the desk. She found some interesting stuff about a dude who was being taunted by a demon."

They both look at me with the same confused expression, both holding drinks. Scott replies, "Really? A demon… here?"

"Yes, Scott. It seems that on an expedition into the rainforest this Mr. Robinson's partner decided to have sex with one of the girls from the village. Sounds like they put a curse on anyone who was there. The part that Cindy was just reading sounds like the guy was trapped in this room," I explain.

Patricia looks at Scott worried and asks, "So what happened to the guy, Darren?"

"I don't know. There wasn't anything more in this book after that. He wrote like he was dying."

"Oh, that's terrible. But I'm sure the demons would be gone by now then, wouldn't they?"

"I would think so Patricia. It's been 97 years already," I reply, seeing Patricia holding onto Scott tighter.

Brenda, having seen Cindy in the window, enters the room and asks, "What's up Cindy?"

Cindy forces a smile and replies, "Brenda. I was wondering what you could tell me about demons. I know you have a little bit of experience in that field."

Brenda stands thoughtfully for a moment before replying, "That depends. What kind of demon we're talking about?"

"I am not sure; the man in the book mentions an amulet with a man and a bird whose wings are wrapped around the man? I am not sure what, if anything, it means myself."

Brenda peeks at the book and after about five minutes of looking at the picture, she responds, "That almost sounds more like a guardian than a demon."

Cindy seems puzzled as she replies, "A guardian? But it sounds as if he was tormented by a demon."

"It could be that someone realized a demon was summoned and gave him the amulet to protect himself."

"Yeah, it sounded more like he didn't know what it was for. I wonder if it's still around here."

Brenda walks away from the book, looking around the room and replies, "Well, if that book is still here, chances are it may be around here somewhere. I'll go to the library tomorrow and see if I can find out the history of this house."

Cindy, noticeably more calm, smiles and responds, "that sounds good Brenda. Let's get back outside to the party."

Just as we start on our way out of the room, the door slams shut. Scott jumps back just before the door slams into him, trapping the five of us inside the little office.

Scott yells, "What the hell's going on here?"

"I have no idea, Scott?" I reply, fearfully, as Patricia and Cindy scream, looking around, trying to figure out what is happening.

Brenda shouts, "Everybody calm down. Chances are someone has something to say to us. What do you want?" She calls out to no one in particular.

We all quiet down, listening for any sounds, and after a few moments a quiet voice begins to speak, "it's here."

We all look around trying to see where the voice is coming from, and Brenda asks, "What's here? Who are you?"

We all listen intently as the ghastly voice responds, "The demon is here in the yard. You are reading from my journals. You must find a way to stop it...before it's too late."

Brenda steps closer to the voice and asks, "What's the demon's name? Are you Mr. Robinson?"

After a brief bit of time, the voice states, "I don't know its name. He wants the flesh of the living so whatever you do, stay away from the willow tree."

"How can we stop something we don't know anything about? You have to tell us something we can use against it."

The man's voice shrieks with fear as it states, "You must stop it. If you do not, you will not leave this house alive. All I know is it came from a tribe in the jungles of the rainforest, and it tormented me. I'm so sorry for killing my wife and daughter. I did not know I did it until afterward. This demon held me in this room until I died."

Brenda looks around as she replies, "What did you do with that amulet you couldn't figure out?"

The man's voice cries out, "I buried it in the yard. I thought that's what I was supposed to do with it; I couldn't find anything out about it."

"Whereabouts in the yard did you bury it?"

The man's voice let's out a ghastly moan and answers, "I buried it by the cornfield."

"Where is the cornfield? There are weeds, taller than me out there."

"The cornfield begins by the well. I must go now, the demon is near," the voice replies, hurriedly.

Just as he finishes speaking, the door flings open. An evil howl shatters the quiet of the house, and we all run out of the room, heading outside to where everyone is by the bonfire.

"Okay, everyone, I think it is time we close this party up," I shout out.

A few people look at me, but the majority do not register my voice and continue partying.

Cindy shouts even louder, "There's some freaky shit going on here guys."

Amber calls out from the crowd, "What kind of things are you talking about?"

"Hey, look in the field, are those eyes staring at us?" I ask frightened, as Cindy shouts, "OH SHIT!" Catching a glimpse of the thousands of red eyes focused on us.

Everyone turns in the direction we are staring as Amber yells, "What the hell are you talking about?"

The man sitting next to Amber slaps her arm, and they seem to realize at the same time. Everyone stands up and begins running in all directions, screaming. The majority of us run for the house, but Tim, Vince, and Sarah run to their vehicles. I stand there in shock, watching a decomposed man with razor sharp teeth biting Billy's back, until Cindy grabs my arm and shouts, "Darren, come on! NOW!"

Snapping out of it, seeing razor like teeth coming for me, I run and slam the door shut just as something crashes against the door. Whatever it is begins scratching, ferociously, as I stand against the door.

Gasping for breath, I ask, "What the heck was that?"

Soon the scratching stops, and I go look out the window with everyone else. We watch as Tim is thrown through his car window, a decomposing woman following him inside. Vince is smashed into the ground repeatedly by a massive manlike creature. We watch as it picks up Vince, raising him over his head, and brings him down for the seventh time. Sarah is forced to kneel in front of Scott's truck; two decomposing females tie her hands until she is bound to the bumper. We all stand there, horrified and screaming, as the events unfold before our eyes.

Ted screams, "We've got to get out there and help them!"

"No Ted. Look at what they are doing to them out there. What do you think they'll do to us if we go out there?" I shout back, petrified.

Ted pushes us all aside, "I don't care. I'm going to help our friends."

Before we can grab and stop him, he opens the door and runs out. Cindy slams the door shut, just as I see a demon-like creature come running at the door. The dark creature looks like a porcupine with a warthog face and red eyes comes. Running over to the window, we watch in horror as Ted is punches a demon, but nothing happening. A near skeletal woman appears out of nowhere, looking like she was buried years ago, and walks amongst the demons. We watch as she makes her way to Ted, grabs him by the arms, and throws him to the ground. We cannot hear the words exchanged between them, but we do hear Ted's scream.

"OH GOD…!"

The woman rips his tongue right out of his mouth and throw it at the window. We stand there shocked as a demon pulls Tim, and another demon attached to Tim, out of the car and throws him on the ground. Tim tries to get up and run, but the devil puts its long claw through his back and picks him up off the ground. Another demon slashes his stomach open, and we watch his insides spill out like chunky soup. The woman gets off Ted and walks up to Tim. What I see next makes us all throw-up. The woman begins to swallow Tim's intestines, in one gulp, and we watch them pass by her ribs.

By the time, we've recovered from the initial shock and look out the window again, just as a demon scratches Vince's eyes out.

Scott shouts, "Damn you all!"

Vince stumbles to his feet, holding his hands over his eyes, screaming for help. Blood spewing out from between his fingers, he walks towards the bonfire, looking for someone to help him. We all run to the room with the desk in it. We watch as Vince stumbles around until he turns around and we can see blood seeping from the deep scratches near his eyes and ears.

We again hear Tim's screams, "HELP ME!"

He starts making his way back, touching the side of the house as a guide, and bangs as he moves towards the front of the house. Just as he gets to the porch, the banging stops.

We listen for footsteps, or anything coming close to the door, but it's silent. We discuss amongst ourselves, what we should do.

"Should someone go out there and bring him inside?" I inquire.

No one seems to object to this idea, so we start making our way gradually to the door. Once close enough, I place my ear against the door itself, trying to listen for any sounds that may be near. After listening, and not hearing anything other than Sarah screaming, I leisurely turn the doorknob, and the door creaks as I pull it open. Peering around the door, I leap back. Fear grips every part of me. The door opens and standing just at the threshold is a demon, holding Vince in front of him.

Terry shouts, "WHY ARE YOU DOING THIS TO US?"

The demon grabs Vince's lower jaw, with his claw and begins moving it like a puppet as he speaks, "I thought we were friends. You left me alone outside with this mean demon, leaving me defenseless to be devoured. That is not what a friend does. Why did you leave me outside? Don't you like me anymore? Why don't you come out and join me?"

The devil sticks two fingers through Vince's empty eye sockets, wiggling his fingers around.

"Dear God, stop that. What do you want from us?" I shout.

He stands there laughing, as he glares a menacing look and replies, "I just want to welcome you to the neighborhood. And what better way is there to meet people than coming over and saying 'Hi'?"

"We're just having a party. Please let us go," I respond, looking at his fingers in Vince's eye sockets. He pulls his fingered claws out, licking each one with a snakelike tongue.

Looking around at us as he states, "Oh, I'm sorry. Where are my manners? Would you like to lick your friend, too?"

Patricia throws up, as I cover my mouth.

"Yes. I know you have been having a party. We have enjoyed a few of your guests already. I am offering you a one-time deal: I will take all of you in one swift kill; I will make it painless for you. If you refuse to go that route, when I do get you, I'll cause the pain to last endlessly."

"Why are you doing this to us? We haven't done anything to you," I shout back.

He grins even more as he comes a little closer and growlingly replies, "Oh but you have my dear boy. You see, you are on my land. You have all started the fire of the summonses. So, welcome to the neighborhood. If you choose to come out, I will make your death as painless as possible. Refuse, and your pain will be great and drawn out. I will give you twenty minutes to decide. While I'm waiting, I'll be playing with your friends out there."

Before anyone can say anything, the door slams shut. We look out the window again and watch as the demon walks over to Sarah with Vince in tow. The beast kneels in front of Sarah, and makes Vince kiss her. She screams as he begins using his claws, scarcely drawing blood, and Sarah's screams grow louder. We all turn to each other, in a dazed state.

"What are we going to do, guys? We can't just leave her out there with that demon," I ask, in a panic as I watch him taunting her.

Scott replies, "I know, Darren. But we can't do anything against a demon. Besides, the beast's claws can do more to us than we can do to those things."

Brenda claps aloud and shouts, "Okay, stop it everyone! I've noticed something, and I might be wrong but hope I am not: Did you see that the demon didn't come inside the house?"

Looking at each other, we each acknowledge this as true.

Brenda continues, "That probably means the demon is unable to enter this house. We can use that to our advantage for a little while. We have a little bit of food in here, and drinks. Maybe if we wait until morning we can make it out of here alive?"

Sarah screams again outside as the demon and those two women continue to taunt her.

Wayne shouts while pointing at the activity outside, "but what about Sarah? We can't just let her be tortured like that."

Brenda looks at Wayne and replies, "I know, Wayne, but we have to think logically about this. As soon as we go outside, they could be hiding anywhere in the darkness. We can just barely make out Sarah from the headlights of Scott's truck. We have maybe a handful of matches, and from what I can see, only two lanterns. That isn't going to be enough to stop them, but there's enough of them to stop us dead in our tracks."

Wayne looks at us disgusted as he claims, "some friends you are. My girlfriend's out there, tied to a truck. If none of you will stand up and help her, I'm going to do it myself."

Scott walks up to Wayne and tries to dissuade him, "Listen, Wayne, what good are you going to be if you get yourself killed?"

Wayne pushes Scott back shouting, "That's easy for you to say, Scott! Your girlfriend is standing right beside you. What would you do if she were outside?"

Scott nods and states, "I get what you're saying, Wayne. I would, undoubtedly, be doing the same thing."

Cindy replies, "Why did you say that? You know it's going to be certain death for him or anyone else that goes outside right now."

"I know, Cindy. Truthfully, I would do the same thing he's doing; it would kill me to watch my girlfriend be tormented by that fucking prick outside."

Wayne looks around the room at us and asks again, "okay, who's going to come out with me to get Sarah back?"

We all just stand there, looking at each other, not knowing what to say or do. Finally, Wayne runs to the door and opens it, shouting, "GREAT FRIENDS YOU ARE!"

We watch from the window as he darts towards Sarah. The demon turns around and he looks right at Wayne, hissing at him. Wayne comes to a dead stop, beginning to scream. The devil's eyes glow blood red, and Wayne yells in agony as a woman bites his arm. The demon looks toward the house and smiles, delighted to have a new victim.

"I see. This is the way it's going to be? One at a time. Very well, we will kill you one at a time then. After I'm done with these two, I'll come over and let you know that I'm ready for the next one."

"Please don't do this to us!" I scream, frightened.

He merely laughs and replies, "I didn't do this to you. You did this to you. I gave you a choice, and you chose the latter."

"Who are you anyway?" I shout.

"I am Dre. I am the bringer of your end."

"Dre, is there some way we can work this out so we don't have to die?" I plead.

"Let me think about that for a second...No! So, are you people going to come out and accept your fate? Or do I wait, and kill you one by one?"

He says this as he raises his fingers, one at a time, and points to each of us.

Cindy shouts, "Please, Dre. There has to be something we can do."

"Yes, there is something you can do. Come out here and accept your fate."

"We won't go out there. Please just let us go back to our homes," I beg, seeing the look on Cindy's face.

He glares at me, and growls, "you are all going to die here. There is nothing you can do that is going to change that. You chose, so your pain will be great."

Cindy yells, "Just let us go back home! We didn't do anything to you."

He looks at Cindy hard, his eyes peering at us as he states, "look here, girl. Let me tell you what I am going to do to you when I get you. I am going to peel your skin off, then I am going to lick your eyeballs and bite each one of your fingers and toes off. Then, you can let your imagination figure out what I am going to do with the rest of you. I will see you soon, Alice."

As soon as he says that, we all turn to look at Alice, standing by the kitchen. She walks to the door shocked and asks, "How do you know my name?"

Dre laughs as he shouts back, "How do you think I know your name? I think that would be the least of your worries for right now."

We slam the door shut on his face, and huddle towards the back wall of the living room. Brenda whispers, "everyone, please calm down. We'll wait till morning, and then we'll get the hell out of here at first light."

Bruce looks at Brenda and asks, "Do you actually think that thing is going to let us leave? I don't believe that will just wait until we come to kill us. I think we should all run for our vehicles and take our chances that way."

"Listen, Bruce. That isn't going to work. Those things are going to fricking wait us out. They are going to wait until we think we're safe, and then they are going to strike," I respond. "You saw what they did to Wayne, didn't you? Do you think we stand a better chance out there or in here?"

Bruce looks at me, and answers, "Yeah, I saw what they did to Wayne. I don't want that to happen to me. If we go now, we might stand a chance of getting out of here, or at least a few of us might."

Brenda shouts above both of us, "Okay, look everyone! Everything's getting out of hand here. Let's just stay here the night; we have food and water to survive. If we go outside, it is certain death right now. At least in the morning, we will be able to see where they are. Right now, they could get the jump on us and we wouldn't notice until they are on top of us. Let's just settle down and try to figure out a plan to get the hell out of here."

Bruce looks towards Brenda and exclaims, "What makes you an expert Brenda?"

Brenda looks at Bruce and explains, "Well if any of you know anything about demons, please step up and let me know?"

The room goes silent, and everyone just looks at each other, back and forth. We are all shocked when we look at the window and see the demon, waving to us, licking the window.

Brenda yells, "stop looking out the window. That bastard is just trying to get us rattled…"

"He's doing a God damn good job of it, Brenda," I reply shaking.

"That's how demons work; they try to get in your head, and once they are in your head, you will do what they want. All we have to do is just wait him out until morning. Once the sun is out, we will get the hell out of here, as quick as we can. Just keep talking to each other. I know we are going to need rest, so we'll take turns sleeping. How many of us are there in total?"

Walking around the room, counting everyone, and walks over to Brenda and states, "fourteen in total."

What are we going to do now?

Standing in the front room, watching everyone chattering amongst each other, I notice the light from the wood burning stove flickering about. The screams outside make each of us jump, as we fearfully look around. A bang against the house quiets us all, and we stand there, looking at each other, not knowing what to say or do about that sound.

Brenda looks around and counts how many of us there are. I can see she is trying to ignore the noise. When finished, she whispers, "as long as we have four that are willing to stay up for at least a couple hours, we can work shifts in teams. We should be able to make it through, the night that way."

"Okay, Brenda… who decides who stays up?" I ask, looking around at the others.

Brenda answers. "I'll stay up first. Who wants to volunteer to be on the first shift with me?"

Scott puts his hand up slightly, while looking at Patricia who nods. Scott smiles and answers Brenda, "Patricia and I will stay up with you."

Jennifer nervously replies, "I'll stay up, too."

Brenda nods and responds, "thank you, Jennifer, Scott, and Patricia. We will stay up on the first shift, and then around 1 a.m. will be the next. Who wants to do that one?"

"I'll do it," Bruce eagerly responds.

Brenda looks at Bruce, and then is startled as she turns towards the window. I also look, and see the demon holding Bill's severed head, sticking his finger in/out of its mouth.

Turning away as the demon bangs on the window, howling with laughter, Brenda stands there composing herself for a moment before asking, "Okay, who's going to get up with Bruce?"

Kyle looks around at everyone and states, "I'll stay up with Bruce."

"Cindy and I will stay up with you, too," I reply, as Cindy nods her head.

Brenda double checks with everyone, "okay. So, Bruce, Kyle, Cindy, and Darren are taking the second shift. That leaves Carla, Sam, Jerry, Joe, Alice, and Terry for the last shift."

Jerry interrupts stating, "I have to go to the bathroom, Brenda, but I don't see any place in here I could take a leak."

Brenda looks around, as we all do, and states, "Yeah, this place isn't huge. Maybe piss out the window?"

Jerry looks concerned as he worriedly asks, "yeah, I could do that. Those demons can't get in, right Brenda?"

Brenda thinks for a second and replies, "I don't think so, Jerry. Otherwise that demon would have come in and got us by now."

Jerry looks worried, but walks towards the kitchen while still talking, "Anyone want to join me?"

Scott looks at Jerry with a smile and replies, "no. I think you're big enough, to go on your own."

We listen as he walks across the floor and disappears into the darkness of the kitchen. A short time later, we hear banging as Jerry yells, "the window's stuck; I can't open it!"

Sam yells back, "hang on, I'll be right there."

Sam heads into the kitchen with the lantern, and a moment later returns, laughing.

We all look at Sam, and Jennifer asks, "What happened Sam?"

Sam, laughing hard exclaims, "Jerry forgot that windows have latches."

"Geez really?"

About 30 seconds later, Jerry screams again, but this time he sounds as if he's in pain. We all run into the kitchen, and there is blood all over his hands.

Scott yells, "What the hell happened, Jerry?"

Jerry is on his knees, screaming in agony, but musters the strength to tell us what happened, "I was taking a leak when something grabbed my dick and pulled it off."

"Tell me you're kidding, Jerry. Something just reached in and pulled off your dick? Yeah right, tell me another one. You almost certainly just want the girls to take a look at your cock," I exclaim as he pulls his hands away from his crotch long enough to show that he is indeed missing that piece of him.

Jennifer shouts, "oh my God! Quick, will someone grab me a towel, so we can stop the bleeding?"

"Holy shit, I'm sorry I didn't believe you. I thought you were just trying to be a dick. Here, take my shirt," I reply, watching as Joe passes my shirt to Jennifer.

Brenda yells out, "okay, from now on if anyone has go to the bathroom, they don't go alone."

Kyle replies, "yeah, no kidding Brenda. I think I'll hold it till morning."

Alice looks like she is ready to be sick as she states, "I don't think I'll be sleeping tonight myself."

Carla looks disgusted as she agrees, "yeah, I don't believe I will either. I think I'm just going to sit by myself in the corner."

"Let's get Jerry into the front room and lay him down."

Scott and Joe grab Jerry, dragging him into the living room and resting him against the wall. Joe asks, "Are you going to be okay, Jerry?"

Jerry leans there grabbing his crotch and moans, "I don't know."

Holding Cindy closer to me, as I glance at Jerry who is writhing in pain, I try my best to comfort her as she whispers in my ear, "we're going to die here tonight… aren't we?"

Kissing her cheek, I whisper back, "I don't know. If we follow what Brenda says, perhaps everything will be all right?"

Standing there, holding each other as I try to forget what is happening around us. Cindy squeezes me tighter, "I hope so Darren. I don't want to die here."

"Neither do I, Cindy… neither do I," I answer, looking out the window. I watch as the demons run amuck, throwing pieces of our friends around, as Sarah screams.

Turning towards Cindy and hugging her tighter, I burst out, "I love you!" with tears welling up as I almost breakdown. Holding Cindy is the one thing that is stopping me from ending my life right now.

Joe pats Cindy and I on our backs and responds, "hey, don't worry; we'll get out of this!"

Turning to look at him, as he tries to smile, Cindy whispers, "Yeah…? I hope we do."

Jerry screams again, as Brenda holds his head and Jennifer holds his arms as they help him lay down.

. . .

I listen as Jerry screams while I hold his head, laying him down. All I can do is just watch and hope it's not as bad as it looks. People spread out around the little house, trying to find some personal space. Looking out the window, and seeing the demon there still glaring back at me, I truly cannot help but wonder if I could find the amulet that would stop him. As people find their cozy spots to settle down, there's a tapping on the window as claws scratch against the walls, setting us all on edge. As Jennifer, Patricia, and Scott come towards me, they look around at where the noise is coming from.

We meet in the middle of the front room, and Patricia asks, "Do you think Jerry's going to be okay, Brenda?"

"I don't know; he has lost a lot of blood," I answer as I watch him, lying on the ground, moaning.

Scott whispers, "We should try to get him out of here and into a hospital as quick as possible."

"I know we should Scott, but our biggest problem right now is those demons outside stopping us," I respond, worriedly.

Jennifer looks at Scott and jumps in, "Scott, don't forget Sarah is still attached to the bumper of your truck. Your truck is the closest to the house, but we can't drive with her still there."

"Poor Sarah. Is she even still alive?" I ask, looking out the window.

I see flickers of movement as Jennifer states, "I think she is; I see her moving sporadically. I wish we could just go out there, grab her, and get her back in here with us."

Scott nods his head as if he has an idea coming around, "you know, the truck isn't that far from the house. What if I were to get in and drive the truck to the porch and we could get Jerry in the back after I untie Sarah…"

"That sounds like a good idea, Scott, but that would still take a lot of time and by then those demons would be all over us…or you," I exclaim, looking at the twenty-foot distance between the truck and the window.

"Well, we have to do something, Brenda. My God, Jerry is going to die right there on the floor."

"You don't have to tell me, Scott! I know we have to do something. That thought has crossed my mind a million times already. Do you want to go stand out there and see what happens? All I can see happening is someone, or all of us, dying. I don't want to be the one that dies; I don't want anyone else to die either," I shout back.

Scott grabs his hair, growling as he retorts, "what if I go out and try to get Sarah back here? Would any of you back me up?"

Jennifer looks at Scott, and then she looks towards me, worried, as she replies, "Brenda makes a lot of sense. I would back you up Scott, but I don't know what I could do other than hold the door open for you?"

"Well, Jennifer, you do realize that if something were to happen to you we wouldn't be much help to you, or Scott either. I know Jerry needs help, but those demons will kill us before we get away. I say we just wait until morning and get the heck out of here."

Scott looks at me, annoyed, then yells, "You know what? I am just going to go for it. I am going to get Sarah off my truck, and I'm going to get Jerry to the hospital! Patricia, you stay with Brenda, I'll be back in a minute."

Patricia looks worried as she stares at Scott, and quickly replies, "You make sure to come back to me."

Scott grins and exclaims, "You got it. I will get Sarah and get her in here as quick as possible. If they come for me, I'll just run back to the house. Simple as that."

"I hope you know what you're doing, Scott. Just listen to how they're clawing the house. Do you have a knife at least?" I ask.

"Yeah, I got my buck knife here. Okay, when you're ready to open the door, I'll run right out."

"Alright Scott. I'm going to open the door gradually, so be ready, but please be careful," I state, walking over to the door and reaching for the handle, deliberately turning the knob slowly and listening for the click.

I start pulling the door back, and Scott looks out the crack of the door. Once the door is open enough, he peeks out, and then walks outside with his knife in hand. I watch through the open door as Patricia and Jennifer watch out the window. He finally gets to the truck and unties Sarah. After picking her up, he starts back towards the house.

Suddenly, Patricia screams, "SCOTT LOOK OUT!"

A demon appears just as he arrives at the threshold of the doorway and slashes his back as he passes the threshold. I slam the door shut as soon as he is inside, and Scott drops to his knees. Putting Sarah's lifeless body on the floor, I look to see the slash mark across his back that is bleeding.

Shrieking in pain at my touch, he cries out, "GEEZ…! How bad is it? It feels pretty profound to me."

"It's through to the bone but not bleeding too bad, Scott. I'll find a piece of cloth and we'll fix you right up," I answer, looking at the blood trickling down his back.

Scott asks, "How about Sarah…how's she holding up?"

Jennifer and Cindy check over Sarah and Cindy exclaims, "She's still breathing! Most of these cuts look superficial. I think she'll be okay thanks to you, Scott."

Scott takes deep breaths as he tries to get his shirt off to expose the gash on his back, and replies, "That's good. I just couldn't sit by and let Sarah stay out there any longer."

"You know, there's one thing that is puzzling me right now: how long it took those demons to get to you Scott. They weren't focused on Sarah; they were just worried about rattling our cages and scratching at the house."

Darren nods at me and replies, "yeah. I was genuinely surprised myself. I know there was one near; I heard it move when I cut the second piece of rope that was holding Sarah. If I didn't know better, I'd say they were expecting us to go for the cars, not the truck."

"If that's the case, then chances are they did something to the truck," I answer, cursing under my breath.

"I guess it would make sense, Brenda. After all, the truck's just twenty feet away. The cars are at least fifty feet away."

Jennifer interrupts us, "give me a hand, Patricia. We'll lay Sarah beside Jerry."

We watch as Patricia and Jennifer carefully move Sarah, and I dab a wet cloth on Scott's back.

He moans and screeches from the pain, "God that burns. What the hell. Do they have a fire in their damn claws?"

Seeing the wounds better now, two of them are very deep. "Don't worry Scott, they are just deep cuts. I'll get some more water on those in a moment."

Just then, we ear a series of rapid knocks at the door. We all look at each other, and I stand up to go answer it. I open the door and see a woman with messed up black hair and a dirty dress standing there. The woman, petrified with fear, looks behind her as she shouts, "Let me in, please. I was chased down the road by something. I don't quite know what it was?"

"Yes, of course, come in. How the hell did you make it this far?" I ask confused, as she quickly slides past me.

She looks at each of us, and answers, "I was walking in the yard here and I heard someone screaming. I came towards the noise and found myself being chased. And now, here I am."

"Yeah, I know the feeling. We've been trapped here for a couple of hours so far tonight," I respond, looking at her as I close the door. I notice she is looking at Sarah and Jerry on the floor.

She asks, "What happened to those two?"

Jennifer looks at her and states, "Those things that were chasing you also got them too. We're hoping to get out of here by morning."

The woman stares at Sarah on the floor, then turns to Jennifer and asks, "What's your name?"

Jennifer smiles a little as she points around the room and introduces us all, "my name is Jennifer; this is Brenda, that's Patricia, and that's Scott. The two on the floor here are Sarah and Jerry. What's your name?"

The woman stares hard at us all, then towards Sarah and Jerry before replying, "My name is Margaret Robinson. I hate to be the bearer of bad news for you all, but…"

We all stare at her confused, as she speaks.

"… None you are going to make it out of here alive. You are all going to die here."

Scott holds his back, suppressing the pained long enough to reply, "Hey, just wait a minute lady."

That is all Scott gets out before the woman pushes him down to the ground.

"Before I forget, I ought to give this back to you Jerry. It's a tad small."

"What the fuck is your problem, lady?"

Darren, Terry and Kyle get in front of her as she pushes everyone back with ease. Before anyone can say or do anything more, the woman reaches out and grabs Jennifer around the neck, opens the door, and throws her outside, closing the door and standing in front of it.

"Get away from that door right now," I yell, trying to move her away. We hear Jennifer screaming outside, banging on the door trying to get back in. Everyone able runs up to the woman and tries to remove her from the door, but she pushes everyone back as we all hit the floor.

Unhallowed

Mrs. Robinson laughs as she states, "you are all going to die here. You raised the evil, and now you are all going to pay the piper. Just as my husband has…"

Joe gets back up, grabs her, and shouts, "Get away from that door so Jennifer can get back in, damn you!"

She pushes Joe away from her; she has limitless strength, as she throws Joe onto Sarah and Jerry. She throws me into the kitchen and Patricia on top of Scott.

Scott shouts in pain, "Where the hell did she go, Brenda?"

"Isn't she by the door, Scott?" I reply, just getting my bearings together.

"I didn't see where she went after she punched me in the back."

As we all slowly pick ourselves up, I go to the front door to let Jennifer back inside. We hear laughing as I open the door and see Jennifer, with a petrified look on her face. Jennifer falls into the house in two pieces; first, her front falls inside, and then her back. I throw up at the sight of her falling to the ground, making an awful sound like meat being slapped together. Still looking for Mrs. Robinson, everyone else joins me in the front room.

"Oh GOD. What happened to Jennifer?" Sam shouts.

Carla looks at the body and screams, "What the hell? This is sick. We have to get out of here!"

"Oh my God. Poor Jennifer. How the hell could anyone do that to her?" Kyle adds.

"Let's put her in that little room. Oh my God this is sickening; how the hell did they cut her in half like that?" I ask, gagging sand shaking my head.

We carry Jennifer's front half into a little closet-like room. I close the door, leaning up against it, feeling weak. Everyone else starts looking around for that woman again, but I feel so torn inside, as if I killed Jennifer myself.

Terry shouts, snapping me back to reality, "How the hell did they do that to her? That woman must be a demon of some sort. But I thought they couldn't come into the house?"

Terry punches a wall as Cindy speaks up, "wait a minute. Everyone just wait. That woman's name was Margaret Robinson… isn't that the wife of the guy in the book?"

Brenda nods approvingly, "Oh my God. Yes. That woman did mention a husband too… Does that mean she's also a demon?"

Scott wheezes as he joins in, "I would have to say that woman is a demon too. I thought they could not come into the house either. You saw them as well as I did, and they weren't coming past the doorway."

"Well I guess now they can. Let's just find Mrs. Robinson and get that bitch the hell out of here," I answer, trying to regain a little bit of myself back.

Looking around for any signs of her, Scott slowly walks around shouting, "Come out here, Mrs. Robinson… we want you out of here… NOW!"

"I hear you on that, Scott. Let's just get her out of here before she does something else to someone," I reply.

"Mrs. Robinson, you here?"

"Come on out, so I can kick your ass!"

Alice looks around, scared, as she mutters, "she's not going to answer you, Terry."

Terry kicks a cooler over and shouts, "Well, then you…"

Terry is cut off mid-sentence by laughter, "Ha-ha-ha-ha."

Pointing toward the kitchen, where the faint laughter seems to be coming from, we slowly make out way over. Just as we are about to reach it, however, the laughter comes from behind us, now. Turning around, as Joe and Terry lead us to the room with the desk, we hear more quiet laughter along with a scratching sound coming from the walls. Suddenly we hear a ruckus in the front room and, turning around quickly, we run towards it.

Finding Sarah sitting up and facing Jerry, Patricia asks, "Are you okay now, Sarah?"

Sarah responds in a whispered tone, "oh. I'm fine, thanks for asking. What happened to Jerry?"

"It's a long story, Sarah. Right now, let's just try to make it until morning."

We continue our search for where the laughing is coming from, and after a few minutes, it stops. We look amongst ourselves, trying to figure out what is up. Even the scratching on the walls has ceased.

Returning to the front room, Sarah is on the floor, poking Jerry's crotch, and smiling as he moans each time.

She looks up at us and smiles, "hiya!"

"Stop that, Sarah. He's been injured. Please don't poke him," I reply, confused as to why she's doing that. As I talk to her, I notice Jerry's penis in his mouth. Looking back at Sarah, her eyes are lost and lifeless as they begin to turn red.

"Oh my God. Sarah is possessed!" I shout as she turns around to look at me, and hisses.

"Hey, back off; wait until Jerry is finished giving head. Ha-ha-ha," she laughs, maniacally.

As I grab her, with the help of the others, she starts kicking and scratching at us, yelling, "STOP IT!"

We get her to the door, but she fights all the way. I manage to open the door as the others throw her outside, landing on the ground by the porch. I slam the door shut, and we listen as she begins to scream at us to let her in.

But then, silence. We look out the window and there is nothing. Sarah is suddenly gone, as if she was never there. We continue to look until we final see her: the demon puts her over the porch's railing and begins to hump her lifeless body as he grins towards us. I cover my eyes, knowing I just killed another person. I jump as I hear a thud. He smashes her lifeless face up against the window while continuing to hump her. Everyone else turns their heads away, but I glare at him as he sticks his snakelike tongue out at me rapidly.

Unhallowed

Patricia yells, "oh my god. What did we just do? We just killed Sarah."

Joe, trying to calm her, quickly replies, "no, Patricia. We didn't. She was possessed."

Cindy suddenly looks at Joe, and replies, "honestly, Joe, we don't know she was influenced by a demon. Maybe she had more injuries than we knew of; she might have had a concussion."

Cindy and Joe continue to dispute what happened as the others join in. They reduce to background noise as I stare at that monster, wanting to kill him with my bare hands. His grin widens into a bigger smile as he stares back at me, continuing to desecrate Sarah's body. He draws a heart on the window and then points to what he's doing, and then at me, as I turn away in disgust.

Don. P. Pankratz

Intimidating is what it does.

The three of us sit there for a while, contemplating what we just did. I try to come to grips with what we had to do, or what I thought was right. We sit there and just looking at Jerry who is hardly moving anymore. Finally the banging against the window stops, and the demon removes Sarah from the window. I turn to look and all I see is a trace of blood in the shape of her face.

Jennifer whispers, "Asshole!"

The devil taps on the window, and as we look he makes humping motions. The scratching on the walls begins again, and we hear something coming from the kitchen that sounds like glass on a table, but there is no table in the kitchen. Grabbing the two lanterns, we head to the kitchen. We shine the weakly lit lamp around the room but cannot see anything, so we head back to the front room.

Another strange noise catches our attention, coming from the room with the desk in it. We go towards the sounds, and it suddenly

96

stops. Jennifer looks at me, her face showing concern, and asks, "It must've just been one of the demons moving around outside, right?"

"Yeah, that would be my guess too. Let's just get back to the front room and wait until it's time to get the hell out of here," I whisper back. Looking around, the scratching sounds become more eerie as the night goes on.

Jennifer's whisper cuts the building silence, "are we going to make it, Brenda?"

Looking at her with an uncertain expression, I answer, "I hope so… but I don't know."

We silently make our way back to the front room and sit on the floor by the wood burning stove. We just stare at each other; I wonder what their thoughts are about this shit. My thoughts are interrupted as Jerry begins shaking, violently, and then suddenly stops.

Getting up and heading over to him, I kneel beside him, but he is not moving anymore. I try to feel for a pulse but, again, there is nothing there. A tapping on the window attracts our attention, and turning around we see the demon, laughing at us and pointing at Jerry. Standing up, I go to the door, open it, and find myself face to face with the devil. Little chunks of our friend's flesh hangs from its teeth as it stands there, grinning.

I look away as I shout, "why are you tormenting us like this?"

The demon growls his response, "I gave you a choice. You decided you wanted to stay and hide. I will mock you until your very dying moment. But if you don't like that, why don't you step outside and let me do you in quick, Brenda?"

"It would be a cold day in hell before I do that," I scream, not caring anymore. I watch as he glares back at me and starts to shake.

"Woo. Is it me or is it chillier out here now? I think it might be that cold day in hell you were talking about Brenda. I think after I am done with you and your friends, I may just visit your family. Yes, I might just do that."

"You stay the HELL away from my family you goddamn disgusting piece of shit!" I yell.

"Well, that's quite a filthy mouth you have on you. Maybe I will just tear those lips off and put them to good use. Why don't you just step outside, and do something about it, Brenda?"

Scott shouts as he grabs me and pulls me back inside, "don't listen to him, Brenda. He's just trying to goad you outside."

The demon laughs as he replies, "why don't you shut up, Scott? Brenda knows what she did and knows she must pay for that."

"Shut up! Don't worry, Scott, I know what he's trying to do and it's not going to work," I shout towards the demon, watching as he eyes Scott.

"Why don't you come out here, Scott? You look big enough to take me on. Come on, we will play for all the marbles? You beat me, and I will let your friends go. You lose, and you will watch as each one of them pays the ultimate price. What do you say there, champ?"

Watching the demon, as he grins an evil smile, you can almost guarantee the demon will win. Scott yells back, "yeah right. You would cheat your ass off to win."

The demon pretends to wipe his eyes as he responds, "oh, that's mean, champ. I wouldn't need anything more than myself to beat you."

"Don't fall for it, Scott," I whisper, "he's trying to do the same thing to you...push you outside." I hold Scott back, watching as the demon's eyes burn red. He growls as he leans towards me, the flesh still hanging from his mouth.

"I don't have to make you come out. I will just sit here, and wait for you people to come to me one by one... Soon, very soon. That is when you will all learn what pain is all about... Especially you, Brenda!"

As soon as he finishes saying that, he disappears in a puff of smoke. The scratching stops again, and I slam the door closed, stepping back gradually towards the middle of the front room.

"I know he wants me for sure, but it seems like he has something up his sleeve. I can feel it," I state, looking around at the others, who look at me with fear in their eyes.

Jennifer grabs my arm and replies, "I know what you mean. That monster seems to want us outside so desperately. But why?"

Patricia looks at the door, and then at me before speaking, "I know why. Somehow the beast can't come in, so it's trying to make sure we come outside to waiting claws."

"Oh my God! You forced me to think of something, Patricia. That ghost earlier said that the amulet was buried in the cornfield. I wonder if that amulet is around here?"

I start looking around for anything resembling an amulet as Jennifer responds, "But that other one came into the house? Is that one not like him?"

"Yeah, that doesn't make sense to me either. I wish I had some of my books here right now," I say in frustration.

As we stand there talking, we hear the sound of footsteps across the floor. Turning around, I notice Jerry is gone.

Scott shouts, "Oh, what the hell is it now?"

Jennifer stares, shocked, as she replies, "this can't be happening again. Jerry was dead; he had no pulse."

As we start to move, we hear a woman's scream coming from the kitchen. We run in just in time to see Jerry picking up Carla, with a demonic smile.

Jennifer screams, "JERRY, NO…!"

Scott runs towards him and is about halfway there when Jerry throws Carla out the kitchen window, headfirst. By this time, everyone is up and running into the kitchen. Terry grabs for Jerry, but Jerry bites Terry's arm. Jerry jumps out the window just as Scott grabs his pant leg. We hear Carla's screams as the demons forcibly drag her into the weeds, kicking and screaming. Carla's screams soon quiet to a whisper.

Unhallowed

Looking out the window, a woman now stands there, staring back at us. Her glare is as cold as ice as she begins laughing. I swear for a second, she looks like a demon, but I shake my head quickly; she's just a woman.

"What the hell are you looking at, demon bitch?"

She smiles seductively and replies, "I'm looking at the next one to join our party...Terry. We can play ring around your intestines...ha-ha."

Terry holds his arm while yelling, "SHUT UP!"

The woman sticks her tongue out and licks her lips as she answers softly, "come out here and make me, baby."

Scott shouts, "don't fall for it, Terry!"

Terry looks at us for a moment, then turns back towards the demon while replying, "I won't. These creatures are just getting under my skin."

"Okay guys, I think we're all going to have to stay awake now. This thing is managing to get into the house and pick us off one at a time," I speak up over the distant sounds of Carla screaming. I want to fall to my knees and die, as Bruce asks:

"How the hell is he managing that, Brenda?"

Looking up at Bruce, trying to keep myself from falling to pieces, I respond, "I don't know what to tell you, Bruce. He just is. He won't come through the front door, but he sure as hell is managing to get in here somehow."

Looking over at Terry, who is holding his arm, I ask, "are you going to be alright Terry?"

He stumbles a bit and takes a few breaths before answering, "I think so; I just hope that thing doesn't have rabies or something."

I can still hear Carla screaming outside, and looking around at the others' faces, they can too. A knock comes at the door, and we look at each other as Alice shouts:

"Go the hell away!"

Bruce looks annoyed and also shouts, "Damn this thing! I have a good mind to fight it and be done with him!"

Alice turns to look at Bruce and says, "Why don't you go answer it this time, Bruce? Brenda looks as if she is going to have a breakdown soon."

Bruce bangs the wall and shouts, "alright, I'll go answer then. You just stay here."

Alice just glares at Bruce, and coldly replies, "fine, I will."

"Bruce be careful; do not go outside, whatever you do," I exclaim, worried, as Bruce makes a quick pace for the door shouting.

"Yeah, I know. Don't worry about it Brenda!"

As he walks towards the door, all I can feel is that it's another one of the demon's tricks. Bruce opens the door, and sure enough the demon is standing there again.

"What the fuck do you want, asshole?" Bruce greets him.

The demon replies, "I just wanted to let you know that Carla is enjoying every moment of what she's getting. Are you sure you don't want to come join her? She has a big orgy planned right now, and you are all invited."

We watch in horror as Bruce grabs the demon, and the demon pulls him out of the house shouting, "look at your friends, Bruce. Did you truly think your anger was stronger than me? You are mine now; kiss my feet."

We all run towards the door as we hear to Bruce shouting, "Fuck you!"

The evilness in the devil's eyes shows as he growls and replies, "is that what you actually want, Bruce? I can help you with that you know… you see this finger? This fist? You'll be feeling that in a second, just hang on."

We watch, in disgust, as the demon shoves his hand down Bruce's throat, as teeth fly out of Bruce's mouth. Bruce jerks around and has a look of fear on his face as he begins to turn blue. The devil turns towards the rest of us, and shouts, "Oh yeah. Now we're really fucking, aren't we, Bruce? You are taking every little bit of my arm down your throat. I do not know any women that could do that as good as you. How about we go a bit further? Nod your head yes… there you go." He pats Bruce on his head with his other hand while watching us.

"I can already feel your intestines. Let's go a bit further. Oh, what do we have here? There are two of them, and they feel weirdly shaped. I'll just have to pull them out and see what they are."

We watch as Bruce's lifeless body falls to the ground, blood coming out of his mouth and nose. The demon looks at us and throws what he is holding into the house. He leans over, grabs Bruce by the leg, and drags him off, humming pleasantly as we star in horror.

I run to the door yelling, "WHY THE HELL DID YOU DO THAT?"

He stops and let's go of Bruce's leg. Turning around to look at me, he comes walking back with an evil smile, stopping at the door. His glare makes me want to run and hide, but I stand there.

"I already told you why," he responds.

"Just let us leave," I beg as he grins, holding his bloody arm towards me.

"I am not holding you inside the house; you are free to leave anytime you like."

"You're going to kill us if we leave," I shout, as his grin grows.

"Yes, and not painlessly either. I'm going to make your death last a lifetime."

I close the door quickly and fall to the ground, weeping. Cindy helps me to my feet again and whispers in my ear, "don't worry, Brenda. We'll be alright."

Trying to compose myself as I squeeze Cindy's hand, I take a deep breath looking at everyone.

"We're not going to make it until morning at this rate, so we have to start thinking smart. This demon is running circles around us already," I state, quietly.

Scott sarcastically replies, "well, duh. Do we have any other heroes that want to try to take on this demon? I mean you are sure making his life easier. This goddamn thing is smart; It already got Carla."

"Okay, just calm down Scott. Let's try to figure out a way that we can make it till the morning and get the hell out of here," I answer back, as Scott looks at me confused.

"That's easier said than done. This thing is ripping us apart, one by one. Everything we think we know about it changes so suddenly. I don't know if this thing can get in here or not, but it sure as hell is sending evil in its place."

"Yes, Scott, I know. I think we better all stick together in the living room for the rest of the night. I don't want anyone else dying because of this thing," I reply, trying not to lose my cool, as we stand closer to each other.

Joe steps closer and asks, "Brenda, do we know anything for sure about it?"

"What we know for sure is that this demon is managing to pick us off one by one. We are aware it is from hell. It seems as if it cannot come inside the house, but yet still manages to get us. Lastly, we know that there may or may not be an amulet around here that could help us," I recap, shrugging my shoulders.

Darren looks both confused and worried as he replies, "what kind of amulet?"

"The kind that may or may not stop this. I don't know for sure Darren," I answer, trying to clear my head.

"Is it in this house? Maybe we can look for it?"

"I don't know Darren."

"Let's check the cupboards; perhaps it's in this place and we might be able to use against him."

"Darren… are you okay?" I ask. He looks as if he's hiding something.

Scott Looks between Darren and I and asks, "What's going on, Brenda?"

Leaning towards Scott, I whisper, "I think Darren is hiding something."

Scott at my face, and nods in agreeance.

We head back to the kitchen with the lanterns and try to see if we can find anything useful. After about thirty minutes of searching, Kyle finds a hidden door in the floor.

The scratching on the walls begins again along with the tapping on the windows as Kyle asks the group, "Should we open it?"

Alice backs away stating, "I'm sure as hell not going down there. One of you can, but I'm not."

"Nobody's asking you to Alice, but someone should go take a look at least," Kyle responds.

Sam looks towards me and shrugs, "I'll go down and take a look since nobody else seems to want to."

Kyle opens the door, and stand there ready for a fight, as the smell of mold wafts up from the floor.

Gagging, I ask, "are you sure you want to go down there, Sam?"

He looks at me and replies, "yeah, what the hell. I don't think I'm going to make it till morning anyway so I might as well get it over with now."

Sam grabs a lantern and and puts his feet on the rickety old ladder, heading down to the basement. He begins his descent, and we listen as the ladder creaks from his weight. He slowly disappears, leaving a little flickering glow that gradually fades until it's dark again. We wait and hear the occasional sound coming from the cellar.

Impatient, Scott leans down and shouts, "Are you alright down there, Sam?"

Sam's distant voice calls back, "yeah, I'm okay. There are a ton of crates down here; do you want me to see if I can bring them up?"

"Do you need someone down there to give you a hand?" Scott replies.

"Yeah, maybe. God, it smells awful down here."

Scott is getting ready to go down as Joe walks towards the ladder and intervenes, "I'll go down. You're hurt man, just relax."

Scott concedes and shouts back to Sam, "Joe's coming down to give you a hand; you might want to bring the light back over here a bit."

"Okay, I'll be right back over there."

We see the light starting to come back over to the hole, and finally Joe heads down the ladder. They both disappear, and a short time later reappears holding a 2-foot crate, that they pass it up to the rest of us. Soon enough there are about 12 boxes upstairs.

"Okay, I think that's enough crates. Why don't you guys come up and we'll see what's in them." Joe yells.

"Okay, but you might want to come check this out after, Brenda. It looks like something tried to scratch its way out of here."

"What do you mean it tried to scratch its way out of here?" I ask, confused.

"You'll have to take a look for yourself. I don't actually know much about this kind of thing."

"I'll come down right now, and you guys can show me what you're talking about," I respond as I start down the ladder.

The light comes closer again as I make my way down the rickety old ladder.

"Holy cow does it ever smell bad down here. Geez, I thought it was bad smelling from upstairs. Okay, where is this thing?"

Joe points the way, as he replies, "this way. You will see what I mean when you see it. It looks like someone was maybe put down here and couldn't get back out."

"Holy cow. I see what you mean. Those aren't animal claw marks, they're from human hands. I wonder if there's a body down here," I wonder out loud, while glancing around.

"We didn't see any signs of a body down here. Maybe someone was just put down here as a punishment years ago?"

"That's possible; these marks look pretty old to me. Well, let's get back upstairs and check out those crates. Maybe if we make it through the night we can figure out what the hell those claw marks are," I reply, feeling uneasy about the basement.

We make our way to the rickety old ladder again, and head back up to the main floor to join everyone in the main room again, surrounded by the crates.

"Does anyone have anything to open up these boxes?"

Scott reaches around himself and pulls out a knife, "this should work."

"Good, I thought you dropped it outside. Let's give it a shot and see what's inside here," I reply.

Scott takes his knife and starts prying the crate open. We remove some of the straw, and inside are some plates. We continue to open the boxes and find many household things. The last container we open is marked with four different countries, including Africa. When opened, we remove some of the straw to uncover six figurines lying beside each other. We take them out and realize two are gold, and the remaining are silver, bronze, copper, and tin.

"What the hell are these things anyway?" Joe asks.

"Bring the light a little closer. These figures look almost hand-carved; I'm not sure what these things are supposed to be, but I wonder if there are more of them in those crates downstairs," I respond.

"Well, we can take a lantern downstairs with Scott's knife and open them up there," Sam suggests.

"Yeah, that sounds like a good idea. We'll head back downstairs; who wants to come with?" I ask.

Cindy makes a face and replies, "you guys should just go downstairs since you're accustomed to that smell anyway."

Joe laughs, "okay, fine; we'll go back downstairs again."

Just as we are standing up, the demon scares the shit out of me by tapping on the window again. We all jump back, as it starts laughing at us. We head back downstairs while the others watch the demon through the window. When we get downstairs again, we start opening up crates and find more household items. We get to one crate that it is larger than the rest, but just as we begin to lift it open, we start hearing that scratching sound again. We shine the lantern all around, trying to make out what is down here with us, but we cannot see anything, so we go back to open up the crate. We hear someone scream from upstairs, so we head back as fast as we can. By the time we get there, the door is open.

I yell, "Why is the door open?"

Patricia screams back, "Carla. Carla...she opened the door. She took Alice outside."

Joe shouts, "Christ! So Alice is out there too?"

Unhallowed

"Yes. Carla opened the door and Alice was standing maybe a foot away. Carla just grabbed her and dragged her outside."

Just messing with you.

Heading to the open door slowly, just in case anyone is waiting, I look around for any signs of Alice, but I can't see anything. Closing the door and heading over to the window, I look outside, also not seeing anything.

Cindy asks through sobs, "Do you see her, Brenda?"

"No, I can't see her," I answer, tearing up.

Wiping my eyes, I look around. Everyone looks demoralized including me by this point. I'm trying to stay strong, but seemingly failing.

In a whisper, I speak up, "okay… we better get something in front of that door, so that does not happen again. This demon is getting too damn smart. It seems to be using us as well."

"Yeah, that sounds like a good idea," Scott replies.

We start piling the crates in front of the door until we can hardly get it to move.

"There, that should make sure that nobody gets in here. So, what did you guys find downstairs?" Darren asks.

"We were just opening up the bigger crate when we heard the scream. Otherwise, we just found more dishes and other household things," I answer.

"So, nothing that's going to help us too much?" Cindy asks.

"Not so far unless you want to throw dishes at it," I reply, looking as Cindy tries to draw a smile.

"I don't think that would help us too much Brenda."

"I don't think that would help us too much either, Cindy. I hope that there's something in that bigger crate that we can use against it. Otherwise, we only have a few more hours until sunrise, and then maybe we can get the hell out of this place," I respond.

"Okay, well let us know what you find when you open it."

"We will as soon as we open it. You guys just watch out for each other; this demon is something else completely," I address the whole group.

"Yes, we figured that already. We won't let each other out of our sights," Darren replies.

We start back down into the cellar and walk back over to the crate. Noises like someone digging catch our attention, and Joe moves the lantern around trying to look for anything moving. We begin prying the crate, and when it is finally open we remove some of the packings around it. I pull a coffin-like object out of the crate and stare at it closely.

As Joe brings the light closer, he looks and asks, "What the hell is that?"

"It looks like a coffin to me, but smaller."

"Are these going to be of any use to us?"

"I don't know. I've never heard of a coffin this small… Oh God, I bet this was a baby's coffin," I whisper, frightened at the thought of holding a baby's resting place.

"Well, put it back down. I don't want to disturb a child's coffin."

I put the coffin back in the crate and place the top back on the container. We make our way back upstairs to where the other ones are waiting. Joe closes the cellar door and we move back into the living room with the others.

They all look at us hopefully, as Cindy asks, "well? Did you find anything helpful?"

"No. All we found was a coffin for a baby. We're still in the same spot," I reply, staring out the window, still wondering myself if we are getting out of here alive.

Patricia startles me as she puts her hand on my arm and asks, "Why would someone have a coffin in the basement instead of a cemetery?"

"I have no idea, Patricia. Maybe that's how they used to bury their kids?" I reply, unsure why myself.

Darren shakes his head, "that's creepy in itself."

Another tap on the window brings our attention back, and we turn to see that damn demon is back again, mocking us. I just stare at it this time, and we hear the door rattle as if someone is trying to get in. We watch this hellion mock us, strutting around in front of the window, with drool dripping down his mouth like a rabid dog. The door rattles again. This time, the crates up against the door start to move away from the door, and we all start running towards the door in hopes of stopping whatever is trying to get in.

Carla screams from outside the door, "Help me! Let me in before it gets me. HELP!"

I continue trying to hold these crates tightly against the door even though I want to move them.

Sam shouts, "Oh my God, that's Carla! Hurry, let's move these boxes and let her in."

Sam quickly moves some of the crates as Scott yells, "No, Sam…"

Before I can stop Sam, he moves the last stack of crates I'm holding just enough and opens the door a crack. A hand reaches in and pulls him out the door. We open the door the rest of the way and try to grab ahold of him, and see the rest of our friends, waiting just outside the door for us. We stop and deliberately move back into the house, slowly. They make a hard run for the door just as we manage to slam it shut. The anger and rage flows as we try to keep the door closed while they scratch, band, and ram the door.

Scott yells over the noise, "holy shit! What are we going to do? We can't hold them off forever."

"Just keep the door shut for now. We'll figure out something soon," I reply fearful, as they continue to push the door open a little more.

We manage to hold them off, and after a few minutes everything is silent outside. The demon is back at the window, laughing and mocking our every movement. As I look around at all my friends, I am starting to think that even if morning comes we will not get out of here alive. We gradually start moving away from the door and putting the crates back in place as the demon continues to watch us. He has taunted and tormented us for three to four hours now, and I still have no idea how to stop him. Everything we have tried has failed wretchedly. If I just knew what kind of demon he was, I would know how to at least injure him. If we could find that amulet maybe, then we might have a fighting chance. But that old man made no sense. I don't know what to do anymore; maybe I should just walk outside.

Cindy screams at me bringing, me out of my thoughts, "Brenda? Brenda, are you there?"

"Huh...? Oh yes, I am sorry. What do you want?" I ask, still dazed in my own world.

"What are we going to do next? You're our best chance to get out of here."

"I don't know, Cindy; everything we try always seems to backfire. I think our best choices are either wait him out or hope we can figure out what his kryptonite is," I reply, feeling defeated inside.

"I don't believe that we can wait him out, but all demons hate heavenly things, right?"

"Most people know what kind of beast they are dealing with. I am not sure who this demon is or why he is here. We could try to see if we can find something with a cross on it or try and make a cross and see what that does to him," I respond, unsure of anything at this point.

"I'll see what I can do about making a cross out of some of the wood chunks."

"Alright, Cindy. If you can make the cross, we can see how it affects him."

Scott interrupts us by shouting, "hey! Brenda, Cindy... everyone else... come here and take a look at Terry's arm."

We all run over to where Terry is sitting on the floor, and Patricia asks, horrified, "oh my God. Why is it turning black?"

Terry holds his arm in agony as he cries out, "I think Jerry has fucking rabies. It seriously hurts and burns like hell."

"Take it easy, Terry. I'm not sure what to tell you; I've never seen a bite that turns black that rapidly. Does anyone have any antibiotics on them?" I ask, concerned, watching as pus leaks out around the edges.

Joe replies, "I don't have anything that would help THAT!"

Looking around, everyone is shaking their heads 'no.'

"Does anyone at least have any salt on them?" I ask, trying to think of ways to suck out the infection.

"I did have a couple packs of salt, but there's one problem… they are sitting by the fire."

"Dammit. I'm sorry, Terry, but we don't have anything here to help you," I say, watching him writher in pain. Terry just looks at us and then looks at his arm with a fearful look on his face.

"I'm not going to make it out of here alive, am I?"

"Don't say that, Terry. You are going to make it out here with the rest of us… alive," I answer, trying to sound hopeful.

Terry just looks down at his arm and responds, "Brenda, I may not be the brightest tool in the drawer, but I know that I am not going to make it until the morning. I can feel it; my arm hurts so bad and the feeling is creeping up my arm. I know you are trying to help, but after everything that has happened so far, I cannot risk your lives too. I've seen what has been happening: every time someone is injured by one of those things, they turn around and injure another one of us. I do not want to hurt anyone of you. I would rather get it over with right now."

"Don't talk like that, Terry. I know what you say is true, but you are not in as bad shape as the others were. You can make it, Terry; I know you can if you just try," I reply, not wanting another friend's death sitting on my shoulders.

Joe looks at Terry and states, "Brenda's right, Terry. There was nothing we could do for our other friends, but you just got bit in the arm. Let's just try to get out of here together in the morning. You with me, bud?"

Terry looks at us both, then past me at the others as he replies, "I'll stay for now, but at the first signs I am just going to go out there. I refuse to be responsible for hurting any of my friends."

Joe pats him on the shoulder, "okay, Terry. Just make sure to let us know if anything worsens."

Through a pained smile, Terry responds, "first signs of anything happening I'll let you all know."

"We need all the help we can get," I respond, relieved.

Terry wheezes in pain as he holds his arm and asks, "So, what's our plan now?"

"Cindy is going to make a cross and see if that has any effect on the demon. We are running out of options for how to defeat it," I answer, trying to sound optimistic.

"Nice. Too bad we didn't have any holy water, that would be even better."

"Yeah, too bad we don't have a lot of things. We would be kicking this thing's ass from one end of the yard to the other."

"We are going to let you try to rest, Terry. We'll let you know what happens as soon as we try something," Joe adds in.

Terry tries to force a smile and shifts to get comfortable before replying, "thanks, guys. I'm just going to try to get a little sleep."

As everyone quietly thinks of ideas, Scott suddenly stands straight up, "what about a stake through the heart? I know that's vampire stuff, but could it work?"

"I greatly doubt it. That amulet is our best chance for right now. We know it's buried by the well, but now it's a matter of how the hell we are going to get out there to get it without being attacked?" I exclaim, watching Terry moving around trying to get comfortable.

Joe turns to look and responds, "There's no way we could make it 2 feet out of this house without being attacked."

Scott walks towards the window and sighs, "I don't want to get one of us killed trying to get it. Why the hell did that guy have to bury it out back?"

"I don't know, Scott. Perhaps he thought it would help protect everyone in the yard?" I answer, trying to figure out any reasoning to this old man's thoughts.

Scott agrees, "Yeah, I guess I might do that too if I figured I was in that much trouble."

Joe nods, agreeing with Scott, "Yeah, I probably would too. There has to be something we are missing in all of this, though. Perhaps something that Mr. Robinson didn't say?"

Scott looks interested as he replies, "you mean something he may have thought wasn't important?"

"Something like that. If he brought this thing here, perhaps he had an idea of what it was? I don't know, we can always check that book and see," I answer, hopeful.

"I'm right behind you. Let's go."

Something to try?

"Hey guys, I was just looking at the journal, but it doesn't say much about that amulet other than that it was given to him unknowingly. Mr. Robinson was also locked in that room most the time, so I wonder if he buried it before or after," I think out loud.

"He would have had to have done it before because I'm pretty sure he died in the room, didn't he?"

"Yeah, it sounds like he didn't leave the room once he was in there," I reply, feeling as if a migraine is about to hit my head.

Joe taps his boot on the floor and states, "that set of claw marks downstairs...could that have been him trying to get out?"

"That could be! Maybe Mr. Robinson was locked in the house, not in the room, and trying to get out?"

My mind races as Joe replies, "maybe he was trying to get out to the well to bury the amulet?"

Scott walks over with Patricia and butts in, "the only way we're going to get a chance to see this well is when the light comes up. Hopefully, by then, we can get the hell out of here."

Cindy and Darren hold each other close as Cindy asks, "Should we just maybe try to wait until morning?"

"Yes. I know everyone wants to get out of here, including me. I think our best bet is to see if that cross works. At least if we can use religious items against it then we stand at least a fighting chance to keep it back from us while we get to our vehicles," I answer, still unsure of what the outcome will be for us.

Scott holds Patricia closer and replies, "Yeah, I guess that's true, isn't it. Let's try that first and then see what else we end up having to do if anything."

Cindy holds a barely held together cross, turns to look at Darren, and then me before replying: "yeah, let's give it a shot. Here's the cross; sorry it's not the greatest, but it's all I could make."

"Well let's see if this works," I exclaim, grabbing the prehistoric cross.

We all head to the front door, and I stand there with the cross behind my back. I gently turn the knob and open the door, looking, but there is nothing out there. I stick my head past the threshold of the door, looking and listening, for the slightest movement. Taking a step outside, even more cautious now, I'm anticipating an attack.

Cindy makes me jump as she cautions me, "be careful!"

I take a few breaths before I take a few more steps outside. Still nothing. I look around leisurely, straining my eyes to see anything in the darkness, and I have a bad feeling. I turn my head to the right and see what looks like something moving, just out of sight of the fire, but I cannot make out what it is. I quicken my pace and head back inside, closing the door.

"You alright Brenda? You're looking pretty pale in this light," Joe asks.

"There's something up, guys. I can feel it in my heart. There is nothing out there, but I noticed something towards the fire. I think we better get ready for them to do something else," I answer, even more confused at that horrible feeling inside.

Scott whispers, while cautiously watching the door, "I'm with you, Brenda. Let's try to make sure they don't anyone this time."

Darren looks around and suddenly asks, "Hey, where's Kyle? Kyle. Where are you, dude?"

"Kyle? Holy shit, don't tell me that damn thing got in and took Kyle now?" I reply, wanting to scream.

"Kyle. Where'd you go man?" Joe shouts.

We all turn towards Terry, who is still laying on the floor. He looks at us, looking at him, and fearfully asks, "What? What is going on? Why are you all staring at me?"

Scott looks relieved as he replies, "Kyle is missing."

Sitting up, moaning while holding his arm, Terry looks around with an extreme pained look on his face. He winces and replies, "what do you mean Kyle went missing? I saw him standing right behind you guys not too long ago."

Joe looks around and asks, "how long ago, Terry?"

"Just before you opened the door. That was the last I saw of Kyle."

We start looking all over the house for Kyle, until all of a sudden, we hear Joe yelling from the kitchen, accompanied by a loud crash. Heading into the kitchen, we see the trap door open.

Scott looks concerned as he asks us, "didn't we close that when we came back up?"

"Yeah, I'm sure we closed it. Joe, you alright?" I ask, worried by Joe's cursing, as we hear Kyle's voice come up from the cellar.

"What the hell are you doing down here, Joe?"

Joe shouts back, "fuck, I think my leg is broken. What the hell are *you* doing down here, you sonofabitch?"

"I came down here to do my business."

"Fuck you, Kyle. You should've said something to us, before doing something stupid like that."

"Sorry I didn't want to tell everyone I was going to take a shit... ALRIGHT!"

Scott leans down into the trapdoor and asks, "Joe, is there any way you can stand?"

We hear Joe shuffling around before he responds, "yeah, I think I might be able to stand on my right leg."

"Well, if Joe can stand, we can grab his hands and pull him up," I say, looking at the others.

"Did you hear what Brenda said, Joe?" Scott asks.

"Yeah, I heard, but you'll have lots of weight to pull up. Are you sure you want to try?"

Looking around as everyone nods, Scott turns back to the hole and responds, "We'll get you out of there, Joe! Help him up, Kyle. Of all the stupid things to do, this is really something."

Kyle shouts back, "I said I'm sorry. What more do you want from me? Of course I'll lift him up."

After a few moments, we see Joe's arms and we start to pull him up slowly. After a bit of struggling, he is laying on the kitchen floor, grabbing for his left ankle. Darren and Scott drag Joe into the front room and put him close to Terry. After taking his boot off, it's apparent that he's broken his ankle.

"We'll try to splint that leg as best we can," I say, looking at his ankle bulging out.

Cindy looks at it closely and states, "get me a couple pieces of solid wood, and something to tie it together with."

Darren grabs a packing crate lid and proceeds to break a few longer usable pieces off as Patricia searches for something that could be used to tie them together.

Coming back with various types of string, rope, and clothing, we watch as Joe screams in pain while Cindy pulls his ankle straight.

"I'LL KILL YOU FOR THIS KYLE!" Joe yells through gritted teeth.

Once Joe relaxes and takes a few deep breaths, Patricia places two pieces of wood on either side of his leg. Cindy begins tying them to his leg, and then a couple to the front and back of his leg.

After she's done, she assesses her handiwork, "well, if that's not a hack job, I don't know what is."

Joe grabs his leg and responds, "well, it feels a lot better than it did before. Thanks, Cindy and Darren. Fuck you, Kyle, you sonofabitch."

Kyle shakes his head and shouts, "I didn't tell you to come walking into the damn kitchen, did I?"

"Kyle, you didn't say anything to us. We thought you were taken by the demon. What were we supposed to say? Oh well...? Kyle's not here, too damn bad?" I exclaim, angrily.

Scott raises his voice, "we're supposed to stick together, man. You know what's been going on here as well as we do."

Cindy looks disgusted as she joins in, "you couldn't be more inconsiderate than doing that stupid shit."

Kyle flings his hands in the air as he yells, "holy fuck, take your pills already. I had to take a crap. It's not as if I went prancing outside. Jesus Christ already, screw you all."

Scott walks over to Kyle and angrily screams, "Do you think you could be more of a douche bag, Kyle? Joe's ankle is broken now, so any chance we had of getting out of here is gone. If anything, you just helped that demon out... ASSHOLE!"

"Get off it already. As I said, I am SORRY; I had to take a shit. Maybe one of you would like to have come down there and watched me take a crap. Saying I am helping that demon out... talk about compelling things to the tenth dimension. Do you want me to open the door and apologize to them, too?" Kyle points to the door, looking like he's ready to hit Scott.

"No. You knew we were trying something out, but nothing happened out there. I made it all the way down to the first step. I even made it back inside. Then we couldn't find you. So yes, we were worried that something had happened to you. Take yourself down a couple notches. We were just looking out for YOU!" I yell, feeling as though everything is falling apart, wondering how long it will be before we all just say, "Fuck it".

Kyle looks at my face, and calms down, "I am sorry. Is that good enough?"

Before I can respond, we are interrupted by tapping on the window. We all look, and it is the demon again.

"Why don't we try opening the door again and see?" Scott whispers.

Cindy nods as she looks at Darren, "Right behind you. We'll move the crates."

After all the boxes are moved away, I gently open the door again, and this time the demon stands right in front of me.

He laughs an evil laugh as he speaks, "well, I see you have come out to see me once again. Would you like to take my hand and I will end you swiftly? Or would you like to drag this out for a little bit longer yet?"

"I want you to..." I reply, watching the evil look in his eyes. He is about to say something when I pull the cross out from behind my back and shove it right in his face. He covers his face, screaming a long, pained, and arduous howl as he shouts:

"Arghhh! My face! It burns!" He drops to his knees, holding his face, and I kneel down, keeping the cross in his face.

"By the power of God, I send you back to hell!" I yell, feeling a little more hopeful that we might get out of here.

"Please, have mercy on me. Get that thing out of my face." He begs.

As he revels in pain, he backs away from the door, screaming and howling so loud it hurts my ears.

"You are going to let my friends and I leave this place right NOW! You are not going to stop us. Do you understand, what I am saying, demon?" I scream.

He continues to back away, cowering, "Yes. I will let you and your friends leave. Just get that thing out of my face!"

"Do you promise to let us go, unhurt?" A sense of hope now flickers in me.

"Yes, I promise to let you out of here. None of my demons will touch you. You have my word."

Unhallowed

"Okay, guys. Let's get out of here!" I shout, watching him closely as he slithers down the steps. He hisses at me, moving to the right side of the stairs as Terry, Joe, and Scott all head to Scott's truck. The demon continues to hiss at me while I hold the cross close to his forehead. Kyle runs for his car and starts it up. Scott takes Terry, inside the truck as Joe shouts, "shit! I forgot my wallet on the floor."

As he hobbles back inside the house to get it, a cold hand touches the cross. I look, and the demon is standing up, laughing at me now. He gets within an inch of my face and whispers, "you foolish girl. Did you truly think that would stop me?"

"Oh God, what have I done?" I reply as I watch the evil look in his eyes.

He howls with laughing as he states, "You have doomed your friends. They belong to me now."

I stand there, confused, until someone grabs me and drags me inside the house. As we watch from the window to see the terrified looks on Terry and Scott's faces, the demon walks up to Scott's truck and starts tapping on the window. The passenger side door opens, and Terry runs out of it as the demon follows. Scott takes the opportunity and makes a run for it; we open the door as he manages to jump inside just before the beast gets there.

"Oh god, what have I done? I've just got two more people killed," I wail, falling to the floor, covering my face to hide the tears.

Cindy whispers in my ear, "Brenda, it's all right. You couldn't have known he was fooling around. I fell for it too, and so did Terry and Kyle. Don't blame yourself, we tried and lost. We'll get him next time, I'm sure of it."

Scott, having caught his breath, chimes in, "yeah, Brenda, don't place the blame solely on yourself. We can blame it on us wanting to get out of here. I honestly thought he was true to his word."

Joe hobbles past me and looks out the window, "hey, guys? Kyle's car is still running."

Cindy gets up to look as well and asks, "Did they get him...?"

Joe takes a long moment before he responds, "I don't know? Maybe? I don't know why he wouldn't be driving off or coming to get us."

Cindy gasps as she suddenly sees, "oh God, look what they're doing to Terry."

We watch as Terry is strutted up to the window, the demon pushing his face up against the window. There is a pained look on his face as he tries to mouth something. The devil has what looks like a cheese grater; he tears off Terry's shirt and begins hitting him with the thing. We can hear Terry screaming each time it hits him, and blood with little bits of skin splatters on the window. We all scream for him to stop it, but that seems to excite him more.

Joe shouts, "STOP IT! GOD DAMN YOU!"

All I can do is watch as a friend I've known for years is slaughtered. Looking up at him, I mouth, "I'm sorry." After about two minutes, Terry begins to slide down the window, making an awful squeaking sound. The demon laughs at us as he takes his finger across the blood on the window and draws a happy face. We turn our heads away and look at each other with sadness and tears.

Putting my head to the floor and crying, I yell, "Of all the stupid things to do, I just got Terry and Kyle killed!"

Cindy looks me in the eyes and replies, "come on, Brenda. Don't blame yourself. We all had a hand in this. Come on and get up; the demon is still watching us. If he sees you lose your cool, we're all dead. None of us know shit about this thing, you at least have helped us survive."

Wiping the tears away and sniffling, I stand up, "thanks, Cindy. This demon has me feeling hopeless and low."

Anger? Friend or Foe?

I stand here, trying to pull myself together again, astounded by what just occurred. The demon is urinating on the window, pointing at us still.

"That fucking thing out there is playing us like fiddles. I say let's just wait until morning," Darren breaks the silence.

"Yes Darren, he is playing us, and we're dancing to his tune. This one is on me, I should've been warier about trusting that the cross was working," I reply, feeling shittier than ever, looking at the floor.

Scott looks at me, and replies, "Like I said, Brenda, we all fell for it. Not just you, all of us did. I also think we should wait until morning."

"Yeah, let's just wait for the morning. It's just an hour or two away," Joe chimes in.

"Okay guys. I guess it's agreed then. We'll wait until morning light and then see what we can do about getting out of here."

Unhallowed

We settle on the floor in the living room trying to figure out what we are going to do next, and after about an hour or so, the sunrise brings a flicker of hope. The scratching begins again, and we try to block it out.

Patricia asks, "What do you think our chances are of getting out of here, Brenda?"

"I don't know. So far, anything we've tried has been useless and he always has something waiting for us. I just don't know what we're going to do," I reply, shaking my head, feeling lower than low.

Joe joins the conversation, "I say at dawn we try to find the amulet and make that thing suffer.

Scott looks around and states, "It's a good idea, Joe. The one problem is we have to try to figure out what this thing's weak spot is."

"So far it seems like it doesn't have any weak spots, but I know there has to be something; everyone has a weakness. We just have to try to figure out what his is," I reply.

"Brenda, out of everything we found so far, what are the things that seem out of place?" Scott asks.

"Out of everything? I would say the biggest thing is that little coffin in the cellar and the scratch marks on the basement wall. I would say those are perhaps the two most major oddities."

"Okay. I know why the coffin seems strange down there, but what about those scratches? Do you know why they are down there?"

"The one reasonable explanation that I could come up with is that they are from the old man who used to live here. That's the one thing that makes sense right now," I answer, trying to believe what I'm saying.

"Okay. How about we go bring that coffin up here and take a better look at it?"

"Maybe we better; if nothing else, it will give us another option." I answer trying to regain some confidence in anything.

Scott looks at me, worriedly, as he turns towards Darren, "Darren, come help me get that coffin upstairs."

"Yeah, if it will help us... I'm game."

We all head to the kitchen while Joe sits on the floor in the front room. Scott and Darren head down the rickety old ladder and disappear, reappearing at the opening of the cellar about 5 minutes later. They pass up the little coffin and tell us to wait because there is another coffin in there too. Once they pass the second one up as well, they come back upstairs and we head to the living room.

Patricia looks at the coffin and asks, "God, this is creepy on so many levels. Do we really have to open it?"

"It's okay Patricia. I know it is creepy, but we have to do it. This may be the only chance we have of figuring out what the hell to do," I respond, hoping I am not going to kill us all.

"Who wants to do the honors of opening that up?" Cindy asks.

Darren pipes up, "I'll do it. I have always wanted to open up the coffin of someone I never knew anyways." He laughs, trying to lighten the mood.

"Are you sure Darren? I ask.

Darren smiles as he replies, "yeah, I'm sure. What's the worst that could happen?"

Patricia in a panicked voice states, "haven't you been here all night, Darren? This whole night is about what's going to occur in the next moment."

Darren gives Patricia a glaring look as he replies, "thanks, Patricia. Now I'm surely wondering what's going to happen to me?"

We watch as Darren sits in front of the coffin, just looking at it. He looks at me, his eyes fearful, and then turns away. Reaching for it very unhurriedly, he begins removing the three pins holding the coffin closed. Each time one's removed, it feels like dealing with a bomb as I jump back. Finally, he removes the last pin and grabs the lid, leisurely removing it. We move the lanterns closer as the cover is removed entirely.

Looking inside, Darren asks, "Brenda? Why is that in the shape of a doll?"

"I don't know, Darren. That doesn't make sense to me. I know a little bit about coffins, from the past, but they weren't shaped; they were just empty boxes, more or less," I answer.

"Maybe it was a deformed baby?" Cindy asks.

"That's fucked up. I've never seen a baby or doll in that shape," Scott replies.

"That's it, Scott. Nothing I've read or seen on deformed children has ever looked anything like this. Look at the form of the head; it almost looks like a little egg. Also, the shape of the body. Look at the way it comes off the head and almost looks like a loaf of bread. The legs are screwed up and goes to the side like an upside-down V. I have never seen anything like that before," I reply confused.

Cindy points at the coffin as she responds, "Brenda, did you see the top of the lid?"

"No I didn't, why?" I ask, curiously.

"I would say this coffin was made for someone. Even the top is shaped."

"What? Let me see that. Holy cow. Where have I seen that before?" I respond, shocked.

"I don't know, Brenda, but that is one ugly fricking thing," Cindy answers.

Scott ponders for a moment, and then replies, "that looks familiar; I know I've seen it, too."

"Let's look at the next one. I'm sure it will come to us soon enough," I reply.

Darren moves the first coffin aside and puts the second one down in front of himself. He begins removing the pins one by one until the lid is ready to come off.

"Hey guys, did you notice that these are different? That coffin is made of hardwood and silver, but this one is made of oak and gold," Darren observes.

Cindy looks at them and responds, "What do you guys think it means?"

Unhallowed

Patricia shrugs her shoulders and states, "if I know my history a bit, typically gold represented wealth. Silver said you were more along the lines of average income."

"Sometimes, Patricia. You are right with the gold though. Look at the tiny etchings on it; I'm not familiar with this language, or those hieroglyphs, but I can say they're not from this country," I respond.

"What about that Spirit tribe in the book?" Cindy asks.

"Oh yes. That could be from there. These items are ancient, so it could be."

"Well, let's open this one up and see what's inside?"

Darren looks at us all then responds, "okay. Let's do it."

Darren begins to lift the lid off, and an awful smell emanates from the coffin. Plugging my nose with my fingers, I hope the smell will go away. As the top comes off, a deocomposed creature is revealed with maggots crawling all over it. Darren pushes it away, and it tips over, spilling the contents on the floor. We all move to the other side of the room closest to the kitchen, looking towards the bottom of the coffin. My skin is crawling right now at the thought of what was in that coffin.

"Oh my god, that thing is decomposing. What the hell... OH MY GOD, that smell. I've got the creeps just thinking about it," Darren yells.

Scott holds his nose, "you're telling me; I can feel my skin crawling, right now."

"Someone's got to do something about that thing," Patricia states.

"If someone can get a bag I'll do something with that," Scott says, wheezing.

We search around and cannot find anything, so we grab a crate and put the dishes aside.

"Here, Scott."

"A crate? Fine, I'll use it."

We watch as Scott heads over to the coffin and turns to look at us with a confused look on his face.

"What's wrong Scott?" Patricia asks, concerned.

Scott continues looking around before replying, "That thing is gone. All that's left are those maggots. That thing is dead, there's no way that it just walked off… right?"

Patricia shouts, "What the hell do you mean it's gone?"

Scott looks around frantically, and yells back, "I mean the freaking thing is gone. Not here anymore. Disappeared!"

Joe tries to stand up while looking around, and the rest of us head over to Scott. We stand there in amazement at the empty coffin.

"Is it possible it entirely decomposed once the air hit it?" I ask.

"I guess that might be possible? I know some things oxidize when the air hits them, but those things are generally older than heck too. Besides, there should be dust or something here, no?" Scott answers.

"Yeah, but you would think that there would be something there still? Wouldn't you?" Cindy chimes in.

Scott still looks around as he replies, "you would think so. I guess it would depend on how old that thing was and the climate it came from."

Scott flips the coffin back up and just stares at it for a bit. While we try to figure out what that thing was.

"It almost looked like the outline of the other coffin. Almost the same shape but a little different," I think out loud, unnerved.

Suddenly, the demon taps on the window yet again, startling me. The laughing has stopped and all of a sudden it looks mad. The look in the beast's eyes is of rage now. It disappears from the window and starts banging on the door, frantically. We all move to the back wall of the living room, worried by this change of events. We can hear the demon screaming from outside.

"What happened now? We didn't do anything," Patricia asks, worried.

"We didn't do anything before either, Patricia. I don't know what he's up to," I reply, scared.

"Well, we better do something pretty quick. It sounds like that thing is going to kick down the door," Scott interrupts.

We hear the demon say something, but we can't quite make it out.

"What did you say, fiend? We weren't listening to what you said?" I yell, trying to keep myself together.

The demon shouts with an ear-shattering scream, "I said get out here right now. Let's end this right here. Open up this door and invite me in."

Scott looks at me and then yells, "Not on your life."

The demon screams again and shouts, "get out here now. I have your friend Kyle here. Are you sure you don't want to open the door?"

"Let's see him first," I say, concerned he is going to make me fall for his tricks.

"What the hell are you doing, Brenda? You know Kyle's dead already," Cindy asks.

Looking at her, I whisper, "Yes maybe he is, but we have to try to figure out why the demon is so pissed off right now. Maybe I can buy us a few seconds while we try to figure it out."

Cindy nods and then shouts, "yeah, let's see Kyle first!"

Shortly after Scott starts moving towards the door, there is a hard bang against the window. We all turn to look and see Kyle's face pressed up against the window, alive.

Scott looks at Kyle and then addresses the rest of us, "let's be wary. I'm going to open the door and find out what he wants but be ready to slam the door shut even if my hands or face or any part of me is in the way. You got it?"

"No matter what, that door will close if anything starts to happen," I reply, feeling my heart starting to race with fear.

"Good. Now let's move these crates."

We move the boxes out of the way, and I open the door unhurriedly, moving back just out of reach if case he tries to grab me. I see Kyle, looking worse for wear, and then I look at the demon beside him. I try glaring him down, but his glare is just a little bit worse.

"This is my last offer to you meddling kids," he snarls. "You come out right now, and I will kill you all quickly. If you do not, I will kill you within the next hour. It will not be slow, it will be continuous. You saw what I did to your friends; I will do it a hundred times worse to each one of you. I am done playing around."

"I'm sorry, demon. We want to live. We deserve to live. And we have not done anything to you. Why do you want us dead?" I ask, watching to see if he is going to lash out.

"That's what I do. I kill little snots like you on a daily basis. You chose to come here; I did not tell you to get over here. Now that you are here, you belong to me. I'll make damn sure each and every one of you pays for eternity."

"Just let us leave in peace. We won't ever come back here, you have our word," I exclaim, worried, as he gets an overwhelming glare in his eyes.

"Words mean nothing to me. Your blood is what means more to me. You and your friends will come out here right now and die. You have no place to go. Your dead friends are right over there waiting for you as well. Think long and hard about what is about to happen here, then ask yourself if it is worth it to hide in a house that's soon going to be your coffin."

"We want to live. If this house is going to be our tomb, then so be it. We'll fight you right until the end," I state.

"Well if that's the way you want it, I'll start with Kyle here and add another murder to my list. You will watch him die!"

"What the hell does it matter anyway? I have been watching my friends die all night at your hands, so what one more is or even two more? Do you think that is going to change our minds? I guarantee you it's not going to stop us," I shout out as I consider what I just said.

The demon starts laughing, stopping only long enough to reply, "yes, you have watched all your friends die one by one like I told you. You should have taken the choice to come out and I would have made it quick, but you chose the latter, so now your friends will die... until it is just you and me. Then I will show you the accurate measure of my anger. You will be praying for death after just a short time. By the time I'm done with you, even you wouldn't be able to recognize yourself."

"Kill him. You are going to do it anyway, so why not just get it over with right now. Come on, do it already."

"Fine, as you wish. Did you hear that, Kyle? She wants me to kill you. That's just what I'm going to do."

I watch as the demon sticks his hand through Kyle's chest, splattering me with blood, holding his heart. Kyle's face goes from fear to peace. I want to break down now, but I remember that we still have to try to get out of here alive.

"Wow. You killed him so well; I could've done better, with a high heel shoe."

I can see the demon's eyes burning into my soul.

"Liar. I can see in your eyes how upset you are about me killing him."

Trying not to fall on the floor, losing myself, I say, "of course I'm angry about it. You just killed one of my friends. It's called having a heart; that's what living is all about. Caring. That is something you'll never understand a day in your life, demon," I exclaim, using every bit of my being trying to hold back from crying.

He points at me and excitedly states, "that's right. I don't have to put up with all that bullshit of 'I love you', and 'I'll never hurt you'. All you people are the same. You always talk about love and caring, but when it comes down to it, you only care about yourselves. I'll never have to have that worry; I just worry about myself."

"Oh, I have noticed that. I have seen you care about yourself all night. Just like you, I don't care for these people in here. I don't care what they truly think of me, but right now we are the best of friends," I shout, trying to stand my ground.

He laughs as he replies, "I'll break that bond yet. By the time I am done they will all hate you. You'll be the most undesirable person alive."

"You can try, but we'll laugh at you while you do," I state, watching as the beast seems to get angrier by the second. "Goodbye, demon. I have to get back to my friends," I exclaim, moving backwards.

Scott closes the door as soon as I am far enough back. The demon lets out a bloodcurdling scream and begins to smash against the door. Scott holds himself tight against the door as we hurriedly rush to put the crates back in place.

"Holy shit. You categorically put your foot up this demon's ass. He is pissed now Brenda," Scott says.

The banging on the door stops, and a loud scratching sound on the window catches our attention. We turn to look, and the demon is dragging its claws down the windowpane. After looking at us for a bit, it disappears into the slowly lightening darkness once again.

Scott looks at me, his eyes full of fear, as he replies, "are you sure that was wise to piss him off like that, Brenda?"

"I had to do it. How else are we going to find out what it wants other than us? I don't know about you guys, but I think he wants whatever is in this house. I bet there was something in here when that Mr. Robinson was alive, something that demon wants or needs. We just have to try to figure out what it is. We know, or at least I think, we are aware the amulet is outside. The demon could get it easily outside, so we are fully aware he does not want that charm, but he must want something else. There has to be something in here," I reply, trying to get the image of Kyle out of my head.

"There are a lot of things in here. Do you want to start throwing things out, one at a time until we figure it out?" Darren asks.

"No, Darren. That's what it wants, and once it has it we will be the most expendable people here. Once we figure out what it is, we can use it to get ourselves out of here. Until then we are stuck. We know that whatever it has to be in the living room somewhere. The look on the demon's face when the door was open told me there is something other than me he wanted. He quit staring at me and glanced at something behind me. Let's start pulling these dishes out again and see if we can find anything at all that looks like it doesn't belong."

Oh my God!

We start taking dishes out of the crates, along with pots and pans, those six figurines, and a host of other little trinkets. As we sit on the floor trying to figure out what it could have been that he was looking at, a loud noise erupts from the cellar. Helping Joe gets to his feet, we cautiously move to the kitchen.

Scott whispers, "Do you think that thing got in the cellar, Brenda?"

"God, I hope not. Make sure that lantern stays close by. I am going to go into the cellar myself," I answer, trembling as I make my way to the kitchen doorway.

Peeking around the corner, the flickering light creates as many shadows as it takes away. Not seeing anything that resembles a demon, we make our way to the trapdoor.

"Someone should go with you, Brenda. It's too dangerous to go down there alone," Scott whispers.

Unhallowed

"I've watched too many of our friends die tonight. If someone's going to make a sacrifice, this time… it's me," I reply, recalculating my thoughts.

"I don't care what you say, Brenda, I'm going down there with you."

"How's your back doing?" I ask, watching Scott grimace as he responds:

"Good enough!"

"Alright then. Just make sure the lantern stays close by."

As we slowly begin to descend the rickety old ladder, my mind says, "No don't." When I finally touch the dirt bottom, I am standing in the rectangular lit spot surrounding the opening. Scott makes his way down and grabs the lantern as we make our way through the cellar. We try to listen for any sounds coming our way and hear what sounds like gnawing. Making our way towards the sound, the lights flicker all about us. We reach the corner of the cellar and can hear the noise coming from behind a crate.

"Are you ready?" Scott asks.

Nodding, as he shakily brings the lantern closer, I grab the box and move it quickly. A rat jumps out at us, and we both scream for a second before regaining our bearings. Taking a moment before we continue walking around, we make our way back to where the large crate of coffins was.

"You still have your knife with you, right?" I ask, turning and seeing the light flickering off his face.

Scott reaches around and replies, "yeah, I have it right here, why?"

"Did you notice that someone dragged this crate, where the coffins, about 3 feet that way?

Scott shines the light to the right and sees the drag marks left in the dust from where the crate was moved.

"No, I didn't notice that. What the hell do you think did that?"

"I don't know, Scott. Nevertheless, that was a large crate. Shine the light over here a little more, there's something on the ground."

Scott brings the light over to the left and asks, "what do you see, Brenda?"

"I'm not sure; I'll try scooping more of the dirt away and see if I can figure it out."

I make a cloud of dirt, scooping as fast as I can. As I keep shoveling, and the pile grows beside me, I finally hit what seems like wood. I start digging, a little further out, until there is about a four-foot space dug. As the lantern light flickers all about, Scott slowly kneels down. Judging by the sound he makes, his back still hurts badly. He hits the ground with the handle of his knife, and a hallow echoing sound emanates from underneath.

"You hear that, Brenda?"

"Yeah, it kind of sounds hollow?" I answer, as he keeps tapping the wood.

"Yeah, but it's not hollow all the way through. There's something in there."

"What do you think is in there, Scott?" I Inquire, intrigued as he looks confused.

"I don't know. With everything that has gone on tonight, it wouldn't surprise me if the demon's mom and dad were in there waiting to attack us. What do you think? Should we try to open it up?"

"I don't know.... What to do you think, Scott? You're the one with the knife," I reply, watching his eyes intensify as if he is looking for an inner strength.

After a few moments, he responds, "we could. What is the worst that could happen? We release another demon?"

Watching as he shrugs his shoulders with a worried look on his face, I reply, "We might as well see what's in here."

We start digging into the wood, it snaps and cracks as Scott jabs into it with his knife. We get a few of the planks out before I ask, "Is there enough room, to bring the lantern in there?"

Scott grabs the lamp and starts drawing it towards the hole. I anticipate the worst happening as the shadow disappears. The light begins to shine into the hole, and soon an awful smell wafts up of mildew and we soon realize that it is a skeleton laying above what looks like a well. We stare at each other for a second, and then continue trying to get the other boards off. We get another two boards off and shine the lantern in there again. The skeleton is perched on two boards just above the rocks.

"What the hell Brenda? Why is there a skeleton here?" Scott whispers.

"If I could tell you that, I would be a miracle worker. Look though, the skeleton has a necklace. Hold the light close enough; I want to see if I can reach it," I respond, laying down and leaning into the hole as Scott grabs my shirt.

"Okay, but whatever you do, don't fall in. We don't know what the heck is down there."

"Yeah, no kidding. Whatever's down there smells bad enough. Just hang on to my jeans; I'm going to try to reach down there."

He lets go of my shirt and grabs the back of my jeans. I slowly inch down between the planks we removed and manage to grab the necklace by the pendant. I try to slip it over the skeleton's head when I suddenly notice a book sitting there as well. I reach a little further and feel myself sliding into the hole; Scott grabs my jeans and makes an anguished sound as he pulls me back.

"Stop pulling me back, Scott! There's a book here as well."

After a little bit of struggling, I muster to get both the necklace and the book as Scott yells, "you better hurry up; my back is killing me!"

Reaching up and placing the book on the plank above me, I try to pull myself up along with Scott's help. Finally getting out and sitting there, Scott falls down to his knees and holds his back.

"Shit… that hurt."

Unhallowed

"Are you going to be alright, Scott?" I ask, seeing the pained look across his face.

"Yeah, I'll be fine."

Holding the necklace and book in the flickering light, the book looks almost like it's bound in skin, and the necklace is gold in color. We start making our way back to the cellar door when a voice whispers to us.

"Stop..."

Scott turns the lantern towards the noise, and as I try to see if there's anything moving around us, Scott asks, "Who's there?"

Becoming more nervous as I look everywhere trying to figure out where that ghastly voice came from, Scott hollers again, "who's there?"

Nothing comes back, so we begin moving towards the cellar door once again. We are just about at the door when we hear the voice whispering again, telling us to stop. This time we look around and see a pale blue light coming towards us from where the book and necklace were. As the voice begins to emanate a glow brighter than the lantern, it looks like a young woman from around the turn of the century.

In a ghastly voice, she states, "thank you. My father trapped me here for over a hundred years. When you removed the book and necklace, you released me."

Dumbfounded as I stand there looking at her, I respond, "you're...welcome? Who are you?"

I ask, praying she isn't going to kill us, as she stands there looking upon us with a smile.

We watch her as she shifts colors and ripples like light on moving water. She holds her left hand up slightly and speaks again, "I am Edwin's daughter, Melissa. My father used to be an explorer until he brought something back with him- a demented soul of sorts. An unseen force decided I must die. Therefore, my father agreed to sacrifice me to the water spirit. I have no idea what a water spirit is, but my dad did. After he built the well outside, he brought the dirt from outside into the cellar and then told me one day to put on this necklace. He said I was to lie over the well on these two planks, and then he stabbed me to death. I guess he decided to fill it in so the planks would not move, and put a book over my head which I suppose is some sort of spell book. I must be going now; I wish you all luck with that demon out there. He is not very nice. Thank you both again."

Before we can say anything else, she disappears instantly. We head back up to the kitchen, and find everyone standing there, watching the light creeping into the kitchen from outside. After Scott comes up, he closes the trap door and we head to the front room with our newfound book and necklace. Once settled, I open the book up and start reading.

"June 7, 1899. One of the artifacts I have found is a set of six statuettes, each one representing different deities. I have long waited for the opportunity to see if these deities actually do come to life. My daughter, Melissa, is reluctant to help me with this experiment.

June 10, 1899. I have given this necklace and pendant to Melissa. This pendant solidifies the entity to a mile radius. The one way to ensure the object stays within the mile perimeter is to make sure the wearer of the necklace is suspended over water. I fear my daughter Melissa will not be willing to do this, so I must do the most horrible thing a father has ever done in the name of scientific learning. I must end my daughter's life.

June 15, 1899. I have everything set up for this experiment; I have spent many days bringing the soil from last fall's digging into the cellar. I am now ready to conduct this research, but my daughter seems wary of my intentions. I have laced her food to make her drowsy, and moments after the ritual will begin. I have already opened the casket that contains the demon, Dre. Once I know if this test works, I will open the other coffin, and release Succubus. This experiment must work. I have worked so hard for this moment and hiding all my research from my colleagues has been tougher than expected. Once I have control of the demon Dre, I will be the one credited with the discovery. I have my fingers crossed that this will work.

June 16, 1899. I have done it; my daughter's body rests above the well on two planks of wood. The necklace is centered, and after my entries I will be placing the book above her head as the ritual suggests. The demon Dre has left the casket and I have placed the pins back in it. Only when it is time to put the beast back in the well will I need those six figurines to do so. I must get the demon out of the cellar, it has been scratching the walls up horribly down here. I should have done this at the well outside. I have seen the demon's eyes lurching towards me in an aggressive state.

June 17, 1899. I sent my wife to the cellar last night and locked the door behind her. I can surely hope the demon has taken a liking to her. I have buried her out by the Willow tree, and the devil has seemed to go with her. I am now free to roam this house, but a robbery of my wagon has yielded the loss of one artifact that I indeed needed. The jungle people called it the repurpose, for it is the one thing to call the demons back to their nesting place.

June 21, 1899. I have just finished the enclosure on the well, and my daughter is securely sealed within the confines of this cellar. The demon will only go 1 mile, no more, from her and is unable to come back into the house. I fear this beast now wants my soul as well and it will stop at nothing to get it. Hearing my daughter calling from the cellar for me to help her is most heartbreaking. I can surely hope that she forgives me for what I have done to her, and to her mother as well. Signed Sir Edwin Robinson June 21, 1899."

I close the book and look at everyone, but we are all unable to speak. Cindy gets up and grabs the six figurines, and as she looks at them, I get an idea.

"Okay. We know there's another demon grunting around here somewhere. We also know those six figurines do something to lock them up. I believe those two coffins are the devil's so-called nesting places. Now, we just have to figure out how this is going to work."

I am becoming more hopeful we'll get out of here, as Cindy responds, "hey, wait a minute, Brenda. Look. If you turn the figurines half a turn and pull them apart they look like keys of some sort."

"Yeah, they might just fit into those pinholes. Now we just have to figure out how to get those demons back in here," I reply, wondering the missing artifact is. "I don't think it's going to be that easy to get them back. Worse yet, we've got another demon running around this house and we have no idea where it is."

"Yeah, no kidding. I'm assuming it would be small, but I'm sure it's still dangerous as hell considering it is a demon after all," Scott chimes in, glancing around the room.

We all split up into different rooms trying to find the demon that is running around inside the house. Walking around sneakily, trying to listen for the pitter-patter of footsteps, I creep into the kitchen. Scott and Patricia follow me, and as I make my way in the sun keeps creeping up, giving me more hope that we'll make it out of here alive.

"Do you see anything Brenda?" Patricia whispers.

"Nothing yet. Perhaps we should check the cupboards?" I respond, staring at every shadow I can see.

Scott opens the closest one and replies, "the only thing in here is dirt."

Getting down on my knees by the sink, and slowly opening the door, I look inside and gasp!

"WHAT? Did you find it?" Scott shouts.

"No… it's a dead rat!" I exclaim, trying to stay focused on what I'm looking for.

The light of day, and a hope for freedom

The sun breaks through the windows and gives us a hint of sunlight. After about a half hour of searching in and under everything except the cellar, Scott, Patricia and myself all head back to the living room.

"Did anyone find it?" Patricia asks the group.

Joe shakes his head and replies, "I didn't see it anywhere; could it have gone out the kitchen window?"

"It could have escaped while we were doing other things, that's always possible," I respond, looking around and seeing we are missing someone. I count Scott, Joe, Patricia and Cindy, but where is Darren?

"Cindy, where's Darren?"

Cindy has a blank stare as she replies, "He didn't come out here? He said he was coming out here and he'd be right back to see me."

Joe looks at her then me as he states, "no, he didn't come out here at all. That's strange."

"Darren. Where are you?" Scott yells. "Did he say anything else to you, Cindy?"

Cindy gets a smile on her face, and softly replies, "well... not after I let him have it."

We all look at here, as if asking for her to elaborate. "What do you mean by that, Cindy?" I ask, confused.

Cindy has a glow about her as she replies, "you know... I let him tap love Valley."

"Did he seem upset? I don't understand," Patricia asks, shaking her head.

Cindy smiles, and as her hand slowly moves down her leg, softly replies, "Not really. He was happy until the end. Would you be upset after being relieved by this?"

Scott shakes his head a bit, and replies, "no, but my judgment might be impaired a bit. Joe, did you see Darren come by here at any time?"

"As I ALREADY said... No one came by here. I never heard anything either. The last time I saw him was right before you all went searching for that demon," Joe replies, clearly irritated.

"Cindy? What really happened in there?" I exclaim, wondering if she got into some drugs. It would explain the way she's acting.

Cindy looks at me smiling, while she still runs her hands up and down herself slowly in a strange manner. She almost moans as she responds, "What do you mean Brenda?"

Getting annoyed as she continues this strange behavior, I push her again.

"I mean with all the shit that's going on here, I can't see Darren getting worked up during a time like this," I exclaim.

Cindy looks at me hard with evil eyes and replies, "what are you insinuating, Brenda? Are you trying to say that I killed my boyfriend?"

"That's not what I'm saying, Cindy. I'm just saying that something else must have happened in there."

"You mean something like I wanted him, but he refused to give me what I wanted?"

"I don't know. There's something strange about that look in your eyes right now. I have a feeling we found our other demon… guys!" I exclaim, feeling stupid that I didn't see it earlier.

Everyone looks at her, ready to kill if need be.

She glares back at us, and shouts, "Don't even come near me or I will kill you all. Yes, I killed your friend. I will kill you all too. Now it is my time to shine. Do NOT even move Scotty boy. You will never again coupe me up in that fucking piece of shit thing for thousands of years. I will help you with what you want, but you are going to help me too. You see, he was supposed to free me first, but that old man did not understand why. He decided to decipher the instructions himself... big mistake. You see, children, when he released Dre from his coffin and did not release me right away, he created his own doom. There are six of those pins. You've been calling them figurines, but they are pins. Each of those pins represents a demon. I will instruct you on how to put him back in the coffin. Once he is back in there, you can leave this place for good. There will be only one condition: You are too never come back here again. I need your word."

Shocked as I stand there, not knowing whether to trust this demon or not, I bend to her will, "You've got a deal. I'm never going to be coming back here again."

"Same here. You won't ever see my face around here again, EVER!" Patricia adds.

Scott glances around and states, "swear on my life. I'll move out of province if I have too."

"Ditto for me," Joe chimes in.

The demon looks us over carefully as she hisses, "Good. I will hold all your souls to binding these words together. The demon you have been dealing with all night deals with death. With you releasing Melissa from her enslavement to the underworld, you have broken a curse. You see, many years ago a curse was placed on a particular man. That man's name was Kevin James. He was an evil man, himself; he had his way with the chieftain's daughter. But if you were not part of the tribe, you could not touch any girl unless the chief allowed you to. He disobeyed this and had his way with his daughter anyway. The chieftain then sent out what you would know as his witch doctors who practiced the dark arts of spirits. They painted symbols on everyone who was on that expedition, guilty or not. Each person received a special gift. Two of us came to this man Edwin Robinson."

The demon stops talking for a moment and sniffs around. After another growl, she hisses and continues:

"He misread the hieroglyphs, which were standard for people not understanding the language of the tribe. Therefore, he sacrificed his daughter and his wife instead of sacrificing himself. Had he sacrificed himself, everything would have been back to normal and we wouldn't be here. Now you are all paying for his mistakes as well. You will never get out of here without my help. That is why he has been tormenting you all night. He counts on your eagerness to leave here intact. That is why he was so mad when he saw the caskets. He now knows you have seen something. He may not know how much you know, but he will figure it out soon enough. When he figures it out, he's going to send your friends back in here to kill you all."

Scott shakes his head and steps in between the demon and me, shouting, "Okay miss demon, or whatever you are. Why are you telling us all this? I don't understand. I thought all demons were evil?"

The demon turns into a beautiful princess complete with all the attire and seductively responds, "oh, we are boy. Give me five minutes in a room with you. I would send you to Heaven before smashing you to hell. That said, as I said before, I was locked up for thousands of years; I do not want to share the spotlight with another demon. That is the one reason I have not killed you all right now. I am willing to sacrifice your four souls for my freedom. Don't ever mistake my kindness for weakness, take it for what it is... selfishness."

Scott steps back as she transforms back into her true self, a horrific demon woman.

"So, what is the amulet that we keep hearing about? What does it do?" I ask, hoping she can answer this question.

She glares at me and hisses softly, "nothing. That is a purely decorative piece of art. That is why the old man buried it. He thought it was some sort of redeeming feature. When you play with the dark spirits, you better know what works and what doesn't, or you'll find out the hard way."

Patricia sounds worried as she states, "I see. I'll never play with another Ouija board or anything along those lines again."

"That's right, girl. Always remember that. If you do not know what is happening, do not start what you cannot finish. Otherwise, you might find yourself face-to-face with me."

"Yes, we all understand. So how are we going to get this demon into the coffin? He's much bigger than the coffin," I ask, stepping back from her glare.

She steps closer to me again and replies, "Size does not matter. Getting Dre to touch it will be another story completely. That is where this next part might sting… just a bit. You see, one of you will have to be holding that when he touches it. That means one of you will have to sacrifice your life for your friend's lives. Do any of you have that love for another? Do you have enough respect for anyone in this room to say the words "I'll do it because I love you?"

We stand there, looking between the three of us, trying to see if there is any hope at all. Patricia eyes the demon and blurts out, "I'll do it. I'll sacrifice myself for my friends."

Scott looks shocked and yells, "The hell you will! I love you and you have your whole life ahead of you. I want you to be happy and enjoy your life. I am willing to do this for you."

Patricia smiles at Scott as she grabs his hand and replies, "I can't let you do that, Scott. I love you with all my heart. We may have only started going out tonight, but you have already shown me a passion I did not know before this evening. After all the blunders I have made, this is the one thing that may make up for everything."

The demon claps her hands together, walks over to them, and replies seductively, "oh. Is that not one of the sweetest gestures? A bittersweet end for one of you when you decide. I guarantee this will not be painless; you will suffer an agonizing death, even more so when he fights to stay out of that coffin. Do not worry though, once he touches it he has no choice but to return to it. That is where the gold pins come into play. You will have one minute to put the nails in the coffin, locking it. You will know where each piece goes once it closes. Therefore, whoever is holding the coffin will be dead, but you will not be able to stop and mourn his or her passing. You must get those pins in as soon as possible. Do you understand?"

I watch as Scott places his forehead against Patricia's, and they stand there silently looking into each other's eyes. I wonder how these demons can be so cruel. I can see the excitement in her eyes as she looks at them.

Scott looks towards the demon and speaks, "is there anything else I need to know before I go?"

Joe comes hobbling over on his good leg and shouts, "enough of this bullshit. I'll do it. Hell, it is the least I could do for you guys. After all, you people pulled me out of the cellar. Besides, you guys make too cute a couple to separate by death."

Scott stares at Joe and his leg and responds, "no, I can't let you do that. You…"

Joe glares at Scott and shouts, "don't tell me what I can't do, Scott! I have made up my mind, and this is what I am going to do". Turning towards the demon, he asks, "What do I have to do, precisely?"

The lets out a hellish laugh as she looks at his leg, then walks towards Joe, "oh boy…are all the heroes out tonight. So be it. You will need to be facing him when he comes out, and once he touches the coffin he will begin to shrink. This is when you are going to die. He will be slashing at you, and slicing you in every way, but it will be too late for him. He is going to be drawn into the coffin, and the lid will fly on top of the coffin sealing it. That is when your friends must put those pins in or they will be yet again finding themselves having to choose another to do as you're about to do."

"I think I understand. Hopefully you guys will remember me for this?" Joe asks, looking towards the rest of us.

Patricia gives Joe and hug and responds, "oh, we will Joe. We will never forget you and what you did for us today."

"You got it, bud. I'll name my first son after you, Joe," Scott adds.

The demon howls with laughter as she replies, "What a bunch of sappy suckers you all are. You could have been out there almost 5 minutes ago."

"We have feelings towards each other. We would at least like to express to the others how we feel. I know it must be hard to understand when you have nothing," I respond, glaring at her as the demon looks at me with a cold stare.

"I'm glad I don't have feelings like that. I would puke every three seconds over shit like that. The putrid smell of emotion...yuck. Are we going to do this or not? Would you people like to fuck first? After all, isn't that what you typically do when you're never going to see a person again?"

Shaking my head at this lack of emotion, I wonder how one becomes so heartless.

"Sorry we have emotions and show feelings towards one another. That's just who we are," Patricia shouts in between sobs.

The demon pretends to wipe a tear away as she states, "that is just so sweet. Now do you want to get out of here, or would you rather wait until the daytime attacks start?"

"What do you mean daytime attacks?" I inquire.

She looks towards me again, this time almost puzzled, "what…! I thought you would've figured out by now that he doesn't give up until the last one of you is dead. You think just because you do not see him out there right now that he is not waiting for an opportune moment to come get you all. He is almost certainly watching you right now, contemplating what he is going to do next. You may be able to see better now, but you are not any safer than you were with minuscule light. You certainly do not know a lot about demons, do you?"

"Not really. We've just been learning tonight," I reply, hating her more every second that passes.

She walks over to me, uncomfortably close, and stares for a moment before continuing:

"Well, let me give you a quick fill in. You see, demons are relentless. If they want, you they can get you any time of day or night. Whether you are sleeping, or awake, we can get to you any time we want. You may be driving, walking, sitting, and bam! We can get you. That is why time is always of the essence when it comes to demons. Considering he has your friends too, he made this statement clear to you all. He will send them in to get you. After all, I am sure he has killed more of you than there are of you here right now. You should surely think about that."

"I didn't realize that demons were so determined," I whisper, hoping she'll move away from me.

She stares into my eyes, and from the smile on her face, it seems that she is enjoying my fear. She raises her hand and touches my face with her finger softly.

"Yes, we are very determined. That is why I want Dre in that coffin. I want him to be in there for at least a thousand years, and I want him to feel everything I have felt. If you want to live longer than today, you should prepare now."

Her head turns towards Joe and she continues talking, "they call you Joe, right?"

Joe looks at her, his eyes showing determination as he replies, "Yes."

The demon moves away from me, and heads over to him. She walks around him a couple of times, mumbling something inaudible, before leaning close to his face and responding, "Well, Joe. Will you be able to walk while holding that coffin?"

"I'm pretty sure I can walk... somewhat."

She hisses at him and shouts, "somewhat isn't going to cut it. You need to be able to move quickly when Dre comes around you. Depending on the direction, if you are not quick he will not touch the coffin and you will die for NOTHING. Show me."

We all watch as Joe stands up straight and begins limping around on his makeshift splint. He starts to turn to the left and to the right and even spins around once.

The demon looks amused as he watches him, "now, try it while holding the coffin. Make sure it is facing upright."

I pick up the coffin and hand it to Joe. His maneuvers are a little slower with the coffin than without it.

The demon looks towards the rest of us and asks, "are you sure you want to bank your hopes of living on him? You must remember that demons are fast. Once that coffin is outside, if he fails one of you will have to go get it to try again. You had better make sure you choose intelligently. You may not get a second chance."

"Can we have a moment to discuss this?" I ask.

"Well, it can be your funeral or your life, so go ahead."

The four of us huddle together, and I whisper, "I don't think you can do it, Joe. What do you think, Scott?"

Scott looks at Joe and asks, "I don't know. What do you say, Joe? Do you think you can manage to do this the first time?"

Joe looks at each of us, his eyes still determined, "I know I can do it. Even if I have to scream through the pain, I'll do it!"

"If you think you've got it, Joe, then by all means, you're the hero," I answer, watching the demon out of the corner of my eyes. She glares in our direction with her arms crossed, tapping her fingers impatiently.

"I've got this. After all the shit we've been through tonight, I am going to show this demon one last night he'll never forget."

Patricia stares at Joe and whispers, "alright then, let's do this."

"Okay, we've decided... we're going let Joe do it. We have faith he won't let us down," I exclaim, addressing the demon.

"Well, hopefully your loyalties aren't misplaced. Once the coffin goes outside, if Joe does not do it, one of you will have to go out, get it, and try it again. Do you understand that?"

"Yes. If Joe fails to lock up that demon, I'll go out and get it," I reply, hoping Joe can do it and somehow manage to survive.

"Then by all means, get out there and capture him. Don't let your friends down; their lives depend on you fulfilling this obligation."

Joe glares at her angrily as he shouts, "holy shit do you put a lot of stress on someone who is already stressed out enough."

Turning away from the demon to address us, Joe states, "I promise I will capture this demon and put him in this coffin once and for all."

We move the crates and the dishes away from the door, and open it to make sure the demon is not around. After a couple moments, Joe comes limping to the door and looks outside for himself.

"Well guys, we had a fun little ride. I will see you on the other side. Remember, you're buying the drinks next time."

Joe limps out onto the porch with the coffin in his left hand, and sluggishly makes his way to the step. Once down on the ground, he begins making his way to the middle of the driveway. He stands there calling the demon. All we can do is stand and watch.

"Come on you sonofabitch. Come get me. Now that the sun's up are you suddenly a chicken?"

We see some movement in the weeds towards the Willow trees, and turn our heads away, knowing what is going to happen to Joe.

"I know you're there, come get me. Come on!" Joe shouts louder than before.

Patricia points and screams, "look out, Joe! Behind you!"

The demon comes running out from behind Scott's truck. He takes a swipe at Joe's back but dodges the coffin as Joe pivots to touch him with it. The demon stops about five feet away from Joe, and just stares.

The demon howls as he states, "Do you really think I'm that stupid, boy?"

Joe, in obvious pain, continues to mock him, "I just want to send you home, little buddy. Why don't you do everyone a favor and jump right in?"

The demon glares at Joe and paces around as he replies, "no. I don't think I will be doing that. I see you are a little worse for wear though. Why don't you and your friends just DIE already?"

Joe looks at him, smiling as he responds, "don't worry about me, I'm fine. Actually, it is you who should be worried. I can still kick your ass."

The demon mocks Joe back, stating, "Well, bring it on. Seeing as you scarcely have a leg to stand on. Why not come on over here and show me what you can do?"

"You're so funny I forgot to laugh. Why don't you come over here?"

The demon growls and eyes Joe as he responds, "I'll come over there, but put that box down first."

"No, I think I'll hold it for a while. I'm kind of fond of this little box."

"You hold that then. I will invite a few of your friends here. I'm sure they would love to see you again."

Joe shakes his head as he replies, "you're such an ass. You just cannot come fight me. You claim to be this mighty demon, yet you don't even have the balls to do anything yourself."

The demon pulls his claws out, as he responds to the taunts, "oh, I will do things to you. How did you get that box?"

Joe looks at us out of the corner of his eye and states, "we figured it out, that's how. You want me to put the box down? I'll put the box down, but then it's going to be you and me one-on-one."

The demon's smile widens, "okay. You put the box down and I'll show you how an ass kicking goes."

Joe looks at him and snickers, "why is it I don't trust you? Oh yeah…because your word means nothing."

The demon howls with laughter as he shouts back, "I'm glad you remembered. Don't worry, I will kill you quickly!"

Joe limps slowly towards the demon, shouting, "I bet you will… come on, I want you to kill me."

The demon begins walking back and forth just out of reach of the coffin. He stops for a moment, "oh, I will, don't you worry, I will, and soon."

Don. P. Pankratz

We watch as they stare each other down, the demon carefully analyzing his next move.

What the Hell!

The demon in Cindy stands there shaking her head as she watches out the corner of the window. She hisses as she states, "hopefully your friend Joe starts showing he can do something more than wobble…"

"He will…he's working on it, just give him a chance. Joe is just trying to figure him out," I counter, glancing outside to see the demon make quick jabs.

"You better hope so…otherwise it's going to be the end for you all."

Patricia comes up beside me and screams in her face, "HE WILL…OKAY?"

The demon smiles as she turns her attention to Patricia and responds, "have I touched a nerve there, Patricia?"

Patricia looks fearfully at her and replies, "Yes, I want out of here…I want to go home."

The demon walks up to Patricia, grabs her shoulders, and whispers menacingly, "oh my dear girl, home is wherever you are."

"My home is with my mom and dad, that's my home," Patricia states, removing the demon's hands.

The demon smiles as she plays with Patricia's hair and softly replies, "oh, my sweet…but if that's where your home is why are you here with me?"

Patricia gets an angry look on her face and yells, "SHUT UP!"

"Hey demon, leave her be alright," Scott interrupts.

The demon walks up to Scott and gets in his face; she looks at him closely and responds, "oh, big balls… have you something to say? Let me tell you something…you are inside, safe for now, as your friend is dying to live out there…think about that."

"Enough! Let's just concentrate on what's happening outside," I shout.

We watch as Joe limps back to the porch. The look on his face shows defeat as if he knows it is not going to work. The demon shadows him to the porch, staying just out of reach. Joe turns around, faces the devil, and puts the coffin at the top of the porch. Looking at the demon, he shouts:

"Well, what are you going to do now? Are you just going to stand there, or are you going to come get me?"

The demon heckles Joe and mocks his movements before replying, "I am going to get you. Why don't you step away from that box?"

Unhallowed

Joe looks at the demon and holds onto his leg while replying, "As you can see, I can't walk very well; I would think you would come get me."

"Take a couple steps away from it. Then it's just you and me, one-on-one."

We watch as Joe takes a couple of steps away from the coffin. The demon begins to inch closer, readying his fists. Joe hits the demon in the face as the beast swipes, slashing Joe's arm. We can see by the look on Joe's facial expression, that he is almost done. Scott moved outside the door and Patricia follows him. The demon shoves Joe, sending him to the ground far away from the porch.

The demon shouts, "You are no match for me, human. Now it's time for you to feel the last strike."

Joe lays on the ground, blood spewing from his chest and face, and shouts, "even if I lose, I still won. I took on a demon face to face, and you can never take that away from me."

The demon looks confused as he replies, "Why would I want to take that away from you? After all, you will be dead and I will still be here. Your frivolous words mean nothing to me. They are just the dying man's chance to make himself feel better."

Joe spits out some blood as he replies, "I don't have to make myself feel better; I know I'm better than you."

The devil walks towards him, "oh yes, and what's next? Are you going to be bargaining for your life soon? Oh please Mr. Dre, let me live? I will do anything you say, just let me live one more day."

Joe spits more blood towards the demon as he shouts, "no. Why would I beg? You aren't worth shit."

Dre walks ever closer as he replies, "why? I don't know. Maybe because I'm going to be the one who sends you to hell."

I stand there, watching them talk back and forth, while Scott grabs the coffin and heads down the stairs. Patricia follows behind, but the demon in Cindy holds me back from helping. As they creep towards the demon, I am ready the tell them to stop, when the devil turns around and looks at them.

The demon yells out, "What do you two think you are going to do with that? I'll tell you what you're going to do... nothing!"

"You're going back to hell, and I'm going to send you there myself," Scott shouts in response.

Scott starts to run towards him, but the demon side steps him easily, slashing his throat on the way by. Scott falls to the ground, and the coffin hits Joe in the leg causing him to yell out. Patricia stands, petrified, as the demon walks over to her.

Pulling away from the demon in the house and running outside, I grab Patricia and we run back into the house. The devil follows us to the doorway, smiling as he addresses us, "oh, my dear, why didn't you just stay out here? You're going to have to come out of there soon, and that's when I'm going to be here, waiting for you. The three of you have no place to go, and soon you will feel a dying need to come out. I have to go deal with your friend, but I'll be back"

Unhallowed

I watch as he heads back towards Joe, and Patricia screams out Scott's name. She runs out of the house and towards the devil, hitting him on the back. He turns around and backhands her onto the ground. Joe grabs the coffin and touches the beast's leg with it as he's momentarily. The monster turns back to Joe, stunned, and lets a hellish scream out. The demon swipes Joe in the chest with its claws rapidly, sending him to the ground, coughing up blood profusely. The devil takes another swipe and another, until Joe's head falls limp, and hits the ground for the last time. The beast leaves him for dead and turns his attention towards Patricia.

"Why isn't he going into the coffin?" I exclaim, looking at the demon who is watching with a smile.

She looks over at me and smirks, "probably because he didn't do it right. If he did, that demon would be in there by now. You should get your friend out there to do it right."

"You said all he had to do was touch him with it. That's what you said!" I scream at her.

She glares at me and states, "yes, I did. I also said Dre had to run into it. That's why I told you I did not think Joe was right for the job. Now it's down to you two to get the job done."

"Why won't you help us?" I ask, feeling an urge to kill her.

She looks at Dre and replies, "I can't. Dre will know it's me if I walk out of this house, and then he will never go near that coffin. That's why I made it very clear: it has to be one of you."

I watch as the demon nears Patricia, his cold-eyed stare peering into her soul. She screams, "please, don't hurt me!"

Dre leans towards Patricia and shouts, "I'm going to do more than hurt you, little girl. Get up. If want someone in that coffin so bad, I can make that happen. I'll put you in there, how's that sound to you? You will be the one in that coffin, and you can spend an eternity cramped up."

Patricia pleads, in tears now, "no, please don't. I don't want to die."

Dre smiles as he coolly corrects her, "oh my dear, you won't die; you'll suffer, but you won't die. Let's go."

Just as I start making my way towards the coffin, rain begins to fall from the sky, quickly turning into a downpour. I can hardly make out what is going on outside with how heavy the rain is falling. I step outside, and just barely make out the demon dragging Patricia towards the coffin to the soundtrack of her screams.

As they slowly make their way over, I run down the stairs as fast as I can, snatching up the coffin. The demon picks Patricia up and throws her towards me, and I hear her scream as she goes by. Running towards the demon, who is not expecting me at that moment, I ram the coffin into his chest, hard. He looks at me and swipes his claws, catching my back and arm. As I fall to the ground, he continues to swipe. I cover my face and curl up like a baby, hoping to avoid a fatal slash. The rain is falling so hard that puddles are forming all around me, and I hear the demon screaming.

Unhallowed

Finally, the slashing stops and I find myself still alive. Crawling over towards Patricia, who is laying just on the other side of Joe, I ask, "Patricia? Are you okay? Patricia?"

I hear a faint moan come from that direction, so I continue to crawl my way towards her. I am in so much pain, but finally reach her. She starts coughing and choking as she raises her head up, barely enough to get above the puddle of water she is laying in.

She looks at me and asks, "Is it over? Did we get him?"

"I think we did, Patricia. Together we got him," I reply, smiling through the pain from his claws.

"That's good, Brenda."

I watch Patricia trying to stand up, slowly, but the pain in my back is making it hard for me to move.

"Let's get in that house and dry up before we get the hell out of here," I reply, falling face first into a puddle. Managing to pull myself up again, Patricia grabs ahold of my good arm.

We help each other to our feet, our arms around one another, and limp back to the house, looking around for any signs of the demon. We cannot see any so we continue to make our way up the stairs and onto the porch. I look, expectantly, for Cindy but no one is at the house. We fall onto the floor in the living room and take a couple moments to reflect on our ordeal. As we sit there, cleaning ourselves up, it suddenly occurs to me: we forgot the pins.

"Oh my God, Patricia. We forget to put the pins in the coffin," I yell.

"You mean he's out?" Patricia answers, panic in her voice.

"Yes, Patricia. I forgot to put the pins in after he was inside. Oh my God, how stupid could I be?" I shout.

"It's not your fault, Brenda. There was so much going on, even I forgot about that."

"Yeah, but I should have remembered. I know now that I have assuredly doomed us both. There is no way he is going to fall for that again," I exclaim, looking out the door, as the pain seems to increase in my arm and back.

Patricia tries reassuring me by saying, "that's okay, Brenda, we'll get him... we'll just sit here for a bit and try to regain our bearings. It will be alright."

"They died in vain because of my stupidity. Now this demon is going to be even madder than before."

"It will be okay," she says again, "together we will defeat this demon. We will be getting out of here... together."

Looking at Patricia, I force out a smile, "maybe, but I've failed myself, you, and our friends all because I forgot one little thing. The one thing that would have ensured we could get out of here alive. I can't believe I was stupid enough to forget that," I scream in frustration.

"Its okay, Brenda. We all make mistakes like that at one time or another, it's only human."

Hearing footsteps coming from the kitchen, I see the demon walking towards us.

Unhallowed

Looking down at us on the floor she asks, "from listening to you two talk, I assume you have not completed the task?"

"No, I forgot about the pins. I am so sorry," I answer, quietly putting my head on the floor.

The demon hisses as she responds, "I told you to make sure you understood everything. Your friends died, and now you will have to choose which of you is going to retrieve the coffin. At least you got him in the coffin...the rain tells me so."

"What do you mean the rain says so?" I ask, lifting my head up and looking at the demon.

"When a demon is contained in the coffin, the rain falls heavy cleansing this place of evil. Therefore, you must have got Dre in there. He is most likely free again, but the rain won't stop for 40 days and 40 nights in this area. It will only cease when he is permanently put in that coffin."

Looking at the demon as she shakes her head at me, I respond, "I'm the one who screwed up, so I will make sure next time he is in there. Isn't that from the Bible? The rains falling?"

"Yes, except the holy one has it wrong. When a demon, such as Dre, is sent to hell, the rains fall, but if they escape during their journey back to hell, the showers will continue for 40 days and 40 nights. The Bible tried to claim it was all sinners, but in actuality it is just when the demons are sent to hell. The rain cleanses the earth surrounding the evil. Based on how the rains are falling right now, he's most definitely escaped. There's only two of you left to capture him now."

Trying to sit up, but finding it extremely difficult, I coolly respond, "Yes, you don't have to remind us there's only two of us left. We will figure out how to destroy this demon and send it back to hell."

"I have to remind you because there were four of you, but now there are two. You need to realize I was right and that you picked the wrong person. This time you must make sure you pick the right person. If you get him this time, you should consider yourself lucky."

"Don't worry; we will get him, and this time he will go to hell," I shout.

"You better hope so. I don't think Dre is going to be that kind towards you this time."

Patricia stands up and shouts at her, "we know what we have to do, and will do it as soon as we figure out everything this time."

The demon looks at Patricia and replies, "yeah well, you better hope so because last time I gave you everything you needed to know. We are well versed in how well you listened, and we are aware how well that worked... right? This time make sure you get him!" The demon glares at us both angrily.

Patricia helps me sit up and looking outside the door I can hardly see past the porch. We tend to our wounds while the demon stares over Patrica's shoulders. I cannot help but think to myself, about how Scott risked his life for us, as did Joe. How are we going to pay them back? There must be something we can do to get out of here alive? I wish I had remembered those pins. How could I forget them? Stupid. Stupid.

Patricia looks at me, concerned, as she asks, "Are you okay Brenda? You seem a little dazed."

"No, I'm fine. I was just trying to figure out how we are going to do this." I glare at the demon as she watches us, like a hawk watches for prey.

"Well, I think for now, let's just start a fire and warm up a bit."

"Yeah, that's a good idea, Patricia. We'll figure out how to get him good," I answer, feeling so much pain.

The demon hisses at us, and exclaims, "You two better think fast. That coffin is still outside, and someone has to get it."

Patricia gives the demon a dirty look as she responds, "I'll go get it, Brenda. You're severely hurt."

"No, Patricia. It's my fault that it's empty, so it should be me who goes and gets it," I reply, trying to get to my feet as the world around me begins to spin.

I stumble towards the door, and I just get to the threshold, the devil is standing there.

He smiles as he growls, "ah Brenda, you want to play with me again? This time I have even better things to do to you. You want to try to lock me up? Come out here and I will lock you up in that damn thing."

"I think I'll stay in here for now. You can't get me in here," I reply, weakly, as he glares into my eyes.

"I gave you a choice before. Why not just come out here and accept your fate? I'll even dance on your grave if you like. Come on, Brenda. Come dance with Dre. I will send you to Heaven before I crash you into a new hell. Take my hand, and you will be free of any other worries."

Stumbling back, I shout out, "never! You will never get to me. Once you are back in that coffin I will go home happy. That is the only time I will be close to you."

"Oh, you will be closer than you think. Let me tell you something Brenda, I never lose. Just in case you do not realize what that means, you and your little friends are going to die here today. You want that coffin? Come and get it, I won't stop you."

"Yeah, and the moment I step out there you'll kill me," I reply as he starts walking away.

"Well, if you choose to come outside and get it, it's right over there. I'll be seeing you soon Brenda, real soon!"

I watch as he turns around shortly, and heads out into the rain, disappearing. I turn and look at Patricia, and the demon possessing Cindy before turning back towards the door. If I go outside, I am dead, but if I stay here any longer, I am going to go crazy and likely die from the blood loss.

"Screw it," I think to myself, "I'm going to go get that coffin and bring it back in here."

Unhallowed

I run, stumbling outside as fast as I can, slipping in the mud at the bottom of the stairs. The pain from the cuts is excruciating, but I get back up and start looking for the coffin on the ground. I stumble across it in a puddle of water and grab it while frantically looking for the lid. I grab ahold of something and realize it's Joe's leg. He's half submerged in a puddle of water. I feel around just underneath him and grab the lid. Standing up and turning around, the demon is face to face with me.

His eyes glow red in the rain as he happily states, "we meet again. See? I let you grab it. Now, my dear, it is time for you to choose."

"Choose what?" I ask, confused.

"The time has come for you to decide. Let your friends live or live yourself."

"We are all getting out of here alive," I reply, feeling like I'm on the brink of collapsing.

He laughs and responds, "oh my dear, but you are not. I never lose. You may have this coffin to use, but I have your friends. You see? They're all right here. They are mine. You see, Brenda, I always win in the end. I have yet to lose against a human being. You are all so arrogant, always trying to stay one step ahead of everyone else. I always reflect on the end of the outcome, and how I will win in the end. Now choose. Do you want to live, or do you want your friends to live?"

"We are all going to get out of here alive, I swear it. You may think you are big and strong, but when you have a heart, that means everything. I have a heart, whereas you're just a soul-sucking meanie," I shout in his face.

He laughs and continues, "A soul-sucking meanie? I will remember that when your soul is mine. Do not fight it anymore, Brenda. You know deep in that heart of yours that you have already lost. Your friends already know you've lost. Everything that has happened to your friends has all been by my design. From the first one to the last one, when I wanted them dead, they died. You do not get to be around for as long as I have by not thinking things through. That is why I gave you choices in the beginning. These decisions determined what I was going to do, and you chose to hide inside that house. Just give yourself to me. Fall to your knees and tell me you're mine. Simple and over quickly."

"I'll never say that. Never!" I shout, making a run for the house as fast as I can.

I hear laughing coming from behind me. He howls and shouts, "Brenda, come back…you know you are mine…forever!"

"Stay away from me…" I shout, slipping in the mud, and resorting to crawling.

"I'll be waiting right here."

Looking back as I make out the house in the distance, I collapse on the ground. As I lay there, I wonder if it is it worth it to fight him anymore. "Patricia, I'm doing this for Patricia," I remind myself.

Unhallowed

Getting to my knees again, and forcing myself to move, I push the coffin along with me.

One Last attempt!

I crawl to the steps and fumble over them. Glancing behind me, I see "Jennifer" standing there. Still cut in half, she looks at me with sad eyes as she speaks, "Brenda. You killed me. You need to pay for that. Come back down to accept your fate and let us rest in peace."

Kyle appears from behind Jennifer and adds, "You killed me as well. You let him rip my heart right out of my chest. You stood there and did not care if I died. Look at me. I am dead because of you. Dead. You must die too."

"I'm sorry Jennifer… Kyle. I did not mean for you to die. I truly didn't, I'm sorry." I reply, tears falling as fast as the rain.

"You purposely pissed him off to get him to kill me. He wouldn't have killed me otherwise, but you made him mad. You provoked him. Now I have to live in this godforsaken place all because of you, Brenda. You should die."

Unhallowed

Sarah stands beside Kyle and shouts, "look how long it took you to come get me, Brenda. You watched as he cut me up. You watched as he killed me deliberately. This is entirely your fault, Brenda. You must pay for this."

I put my head down on the top step and sob, "I'm sorry, Sarah. I'm sorry to all of you. I never meant for any of this to happen to any of you."

I break down, laying on the porch crying, as they keep coming up to me, and telling me, one by one that I need to die. I cannot help but feel a heart-strangling pain, knowing it is indeed my fault that they died. I want to run into the house so bad, but I cannot move. I feel such an immense guilt for all of my decisions and their horrific consequences.

The demon walks in between Kyle and Sarah, and addresses me once more, "do you see now, Brenda? All your friends blaming you for their deaths. You must know that it is strictly your fault they are dead. Fall to your knees in front of me and tell me to take you. Then your guilt will be over."

"I...I don't know what to do anymore. Why me? Why do I have to die to make everything right again?" I ask, rubbing my face, looking at my friends who are all calling for my death.

The demon holds his hand towards me and answers, "Because that is your destiny, Brenda. You are the sole reason they are dead."

"I am not the reason they are dead, you are. You killed all my friends, not me. Goddamn it, YOU killed my friends!" I scream, trying to hit him.

He looks at me and softly states, "no Brenda, it was you. You know you feel it deep in that beating heart of yours; it is you who put each of them in danger. You now carry that burden. Let me ease the pain that will haunt you for as long as you live. Kneel before me, and I'll set you free."

I look at him, registering the evilness of his smile, and then I hear someone limping through water, and a figure appears in the rain.

"Joe, is that you?" I exclaim, watching as he hobbles towards me, his chest wide open and his stomach hanging out from a lower cut.

"Yes. You let me go out, knowing I could not possibly fight Dre. You let him kill me when you could have come out and stopped him. You let him kill me," Joe yells.

"I didn't, Joe. You were the one that volunteered to go out and put him in the coffin," I respond in a whisper.

He takes a step closer and replies, "I only volunteered because you didn't. I did it so Patricia did not have too. I saw you looking at Patricia; you were going to send that poor girl out here to die because you were afraid. That is a shame you will have to carry around with you. Shame on you Brenda...shame."

"I wasn't Joe... I didn't... Everyone decided who was going to go out, that can't be on just me. I'm sorry. I wish I would have taken your place, I really do. Joe, please forgive me?" I plead.

Unhallowed

He scoffs at me and yells, "no, I will not forgive you. I would rather piss on your grave than forgive you! This whole night is on you, Brenda. Everything that happened is because of you. Now, accept your fate and die like the rest of us. That solitary thing is going to make you complete again. Go to him and fall to your knees. Beg him to take you. Make your life mean something; let everyone know you took responsibility for everything that happened to us. Come on Brenda, do it… for all of us who died… for you."

"I thank you for everything you did, Joe, but I did not kill you; I did not kill any of you. Why do you so want me to die so bad? I did the best I could with what I had. I didn't want anyone to die. You're my friends, and I didn't want anything bad to happen… to any of you!" I shout out franticly.

Vince appears on the other side of Jennifer and joins the shouting, "friends is something we are not, Brenda. I wish I'd never seen you, because then I would still be alive. You let them bash me into the ground. You stood by and did nothing. You just let them kill me as you let everyone else die. You are responsible for all of our deaths. Get on your knees and tell him to kill you. Make it easy on all of us."

"Vince, I didn't kill you. What was I supposed to do? I couldn't do anything to stop them. I'm sorry you died," I scream at the growing mob.

The demon, in a soothing voice, calls out, "look, Brenda. I am offering to relieve you of any guilt from these deaths. All you have to do is kneel in front of me and tell me to take you. You say that, and I will take you in one swipe. All you have to do is kneel in front of me."

Tears falling, I try so hard to move, but the physical pain and the pain in my heart bear so much weight that crying is all I can seem to do.

The crowd around me begins to chant, "Do it" repeatedly, and I crawl back down to the bottom of the stairs. When I get in front of the demon, he looks down on me with the creepiest of smiles. I look up at him as he pulls back his hand, revealing claws.

"Say it; say the words I want to hear, Brenda, and once you do I will free you from your torment."

I look up at him and all around, the rain falling in my eyes. Returning my gaze to the ground one last time, I take a deep breath and shout, "No!" as I thrust the coffin into him as hard as I can.

He howls and screams, and starts swiping at me, hitting me multiple times with his claws. I scream in pain as I watch him slowly disappear into the coffin. I yell for Patricia to bring the pins as he continues to swipe, struggling to not be absorbed into the coffin.

Patricia comes running out with the pins ready to close the sonofabitch up forever. After a few minutes, Dre is tightly packed away, and the lid flies on top of the coffin. In a feeble voice, I say, "Do it now."

Patricia puts each pin in and when she is finished, carries the coffin into the house. I lay there, bleeding and feeling so cold, knowing I am going to die. My surroundings begin to dull into a quiet peacefulness until I am startled by Patricia.

"Brenda! I'm going to bring you inside," she yells to me.

Feeling a tug on my arms, Patricia pulls me out of the rain and onto the porch. As I lay there, sheltered but still bleeding profusely, Patricia wraps my wounds. Whether from exhaustion or the sheer pain of it, I slowly close my eyes as I lose consciousness.

...

I watch Brenda, lying on the porch, while I press on the deep wounds to slow the bleeding. After a few minutes, the bleeding seems to be under control and Brenda is resting contentedly.

Looking at the demon in Cindy, I ask, "So? When can Brenda and I leave? That demon is in the coffin, and it's locked tight. I'm worried about Brenda, and how much medical attention she needs right now."

The demon looks at me and replies, "I think you and your friend should stay here a little longer. Wait till the storm clears up a bit. I wouldn't want to see you get hurt after completing your task... at last."

"Yes, Brenda finished that. I think she did pretty well, and am amazed that she's still alive," I reply, looking at Brenda's unconscious body.

The demon smiles and responds, "yes, that says a lot about her. When she wakes up I will thank her myself. Or rather, if she wakes up?"

"What do you mean 'if' she wakes up? You don't think she's going to wake up?" I exclaim.

The demon puts her hand on my shoulder and whispers, "oh my dear Patricia. I must explain something to you... lets you and I let Brenda rest. Let's go take a walk outside in the rain."

"Can we go talk in another room instead of going outside?" I ask as the demon glances back at Brenda.

"I think it would be best if we go outside and talk."

The demon helps me up, and we head outside, the rain still coming down as hard as ever. We head down the steps and start walking towards the willow tree.

The demon has her arm around me as she explains, "you see, Patricia, your friend Brenda isn't going to make it. As I said earlier, whoever holds the coffin will die. You see, there is no uncertainty. She will die, and there is nothing you can do to stop that. As for you... look at this. You're outside, and not being attacked by any demons."

Looking at her smiling face, I respond, "no, I guess not. Is there anything that we can do at all for Brenda? To just stop the bleeding even?"

The demon has a sorrowful look on her face as she answers me, "no. As I have said, Brenda will die. There is no stopping that whatsoever. I know you lost your friend... Scott... was that his name?"

"Yes, that was his name. He was my boyfriend for all but maybe seven hours," I reply, looking at the ground and shuffling my feet.

The demon softly puts her hand on my cheek, and lifts my head up, looking into my eyes, "that is no good. You mean you never even got a chance to do anything...?"

"No, we never had the opportunity to even go out on a date. I have a feeling he would have been the one for me."

"Oh, that is not okay at all. What would you say if I could bring Scott back? Even for an hour so you can express your love to him? What would you say? What would you give?"

"I would give anything to have him back even just for an hour," I reply.

"Anything? That is a tall order. A tall order like that requires a hefty pavement. If I were to do this for you, would you give me... your soul?"

"My soul? You mean you'll give me an hour with Scott and then kill me?" I state, looking at her with suspicion as to her motives.

"Yes, your soul. I will gift you an hour with Scott, and after this hour is up... when you die, your soul belongs to me."

"So, are you saying you're not going to kill me right after?" I ask, confused.

She hugs me and states, "no my dear, I would not do that to you. You will have your hour with Scott, and as soon as you pass away naturally, by whatever means, then your soul will belong to me.

I will not kill you, and you have my word as long as I have your word."

"You have my word, as long as you promise not to murder me," I reply, still watching her eyes for a sign of trickery.

"I promise you, I will not kill you. Do you want this hour with your love? Or would you like to just be on your way?"

"I so much want an hour with Scott. I want to be able to touch and feel him again," I exclaim, excitedly thinking about how he made me feel in those few hours.

"Very well, Patricia. You shall have your hour of glory. Make it worthwhile though, this is the one chance you'll have to say everything you want... including goodbye."

"I will make every second count," I reply, smiling.

"Close your eyes and count to ten. When your eyes open Scott will be here. Remember... one hour," she whispers into my ear.

"Yes, I remember. So, count to ten. Okay, one, two... ten."

Turning around, I see Scott standing where the demon was.

"Oh, Scott! I missed you," I exclaim, reaching around and giving him a hug.

"I missed you too, babe. I thought I would never see you again."

"You feel so alive right now. Look, neither of us are wounded anymore," I shout, hugging him even harder than before.

Scott runs his hand through my hair gently as he whispers, "being away from you for this time has been a nightmare for me. I have so wanted to touch you, in every way imaginable. I was so incredibly saddened when that demon cut me open. I knew I would never again touch your skin… your hair. I don't know what you have done, but I am grateful for these moments we have again."

"Scott, I love you more than words could ever say. I know our time is going to be limited, but I want to make every second feel like a lifetime. I hope you feel that same way about me?"

His hand moves towards my waist as he replies, "if our time is going to be limited, I want to touch your bare skin; I want to do things that show you I love you more than life itself. I want you and me to become one."

"Are you saying what I think you're saying, Scott? I want you just as bad; I just wish it had been somewhere else instead of here."

"I feel the same way, Patricia, but anywhere we do it is going to be special as long as you are there. Together, you and I will become one with each other. Your love intertwined with my love together will last an eternity."

"Yes, I am yours; together we will have this moment forever," I exclaim.

"Yes, together."

We lean into each other in an embraced kiss, and he begins by unbuttoning my shirt. He lays me down in the rain and we start making out fervently. I feel like I am in heaven with every thrust. The cold rain feels warm against my skin.

Afterward, we lean up against the willow tree, and Scott looks into my eyes, "that was wonderful, Patricia. I wish it could last a lifetime."

"So do I, Scott. I never want to let you go again," I state, holding onto him tightly.

Scott looks deep into my eyes and replies, "maybe we don't have to let each other go, Patricia. Why don't you come with me, and we can be together... always?"

"I can't, Scott. I wish I could, but you have to go back to wherever it is you are. Besides, Brenda needs me to help her back to the city; she is in no shape to get there by herself," I reply as Scott touches my face softly.

"Why can't you, Patricia? Doesn't everyone go to the same place? Don't worry about Brenda; I am sure she will find a way home."

"No, I was told that I can't go with you. That I would only get one hour with you. She is in no shape to go anywhere by herself. She locked that demon up, and he cut her good."

"I would love for you and me to walk together always. Just you and I together forever."

"We will meet again one day, I know we will. And when that day comes, we will never be apart again," I exclaim, kissing him on the lips.

"That day may be soon, Patricia. I will fight my way back through whatever awaits me to be by your side once again."

"Yes, my darling Scott. I hope that one of these days we will meet again, and then I will never let you go. I love you, Scott," I whisper as I lean against his chest.

He kisses my forehead and whispers back, "I love you, Patricia. No matter what happens I hope you know I will always love you."

"Let's get up and go for a walk," I suggest, as Scott helps me up. He puts his arm around me, as we walk through the weeds.

He looks back and asks, "what about your clothes?"

"Don't worry about my clothes, Scott. Let's just walk."

We walk through the weeds, and Scott looks at me, smiling a little differently.

"Scott, you look different… what happened?"

Scott looks away for a moment, and replies, "oh, I guess when that demon brought me back, maybe I was messed up or something?"

"Yeah, I guess that could be. I didn't get a good look at you after you died," I reply as Scott holds me closer.

"Let's not worry about me, let's make this time about you, my love."

"I just wish I had the courage to tell you before last night that I loved you," I reply, leaning my head against his shoulder.

"I wish you had too. Your soft skin and that feeling you give me inside is something I will never forget. I hope I get one last chance to feel you like that again."

"What are you trying to say?" I ask as Scott's smile grows.

Unhallowed

"I want you again, Patricia."

"I want you too, Scott. Should we make our way back to where our clothes are?" I ask.

Standing there, holding each other close, I feel as though this must be how Adam and Eve felt. Walking through the garden in the passion of just being alone with the one you love.

Scott whispers, "no. I want you right here, right now."

We find a space that has the fewest weeds, and he lays me down. Scott looks at me, leans in for a kiss, and we embrace our entire bodies. As the passion flows between us in a magical moment, Scott grabs me by the throat and squeezes as tight as he can. I try fighting him off, but it is no use.

He smiles slyly, "you're coming with me, Patricia. You see, your soul belongs to me. You had your hour with your precious Scott, and now you will have an eternity to spend with me, Succubus. That's right, do not fight me; it only excites me to no end. I want you alive when you feel my enthusiasm. Yes. I can feel your soul coming to me. Together, our magic will be superb. You're beautiful with that look of fear in your eyes. Soon we will be together forever."

So close.

Still feeling weak from all the cuts and blood loss, I try to stand up. Looking out the door, I see that the rain is still falling. I stumble around looking for Patricia or the demon, but I cannot find them anywhere.

Making my way outside, I stumble and call out, "Patricia? Cindy? Where are you?"

No one answers back. I begin turning around slowly to go back in the house when a porcupine-looking, warthog-faced demon suddenly grabs me by the throat.

"I told you… I always win, always! Let us take a walk down to the cellar, shall we? You are going to love your new home. Did you actually believe you had a chance, Brenda?"

I can barely breathe let alone form words as he drags me through the front room into the kitchen and opens up the cellar door. He picks me up and drops me on the basement floor. Screaming from the pain of the drop, I try to crawl away, but he jumps down and lands on my leg. I hear a snap and am flooded with more pain. He grabs me by my hair and drags me into the darkest part of the cellar.

"I love you young people, did you know that? You all are what keeps us going all these years. Remember how I told you that you would be in pain like no other? Well, get ready for some agonizing pain, Brenda."

I feel cold in the darkness, and a sharp stabbing pain pierces my spine, causing my arms and legs to fall limp. I can't move as I hear the sound of wood.

He laughs as he states, "I hope that didn't hurt you too much, Brenda. After all, you are going to be here for a while. Since you were so kind to release Melissa from her confinement, you will take her place. Enjoy yourself, Brenda; you are now bound to this house. Before I go and leave you to rot here, I will tell you the real story…

What you read in that book upstairs was only one piece of the puzzle. You see Brenda, a long time ago, a team of people came to a village, that had been condemned by all the others for the practices of dark magic. One of these men was Edward Robinson. In the beginning, they came to listen and learn, but on the third visit, they insulted the new chief by trying his daughter on for size… they raped her. After the father killed his daughter, to free her from the disgrace of living with this burden, they sent the guilty party to the judgment of the forest, but he came back alive. Not happy with Abrazz's judgment, the people turned to their dark magic."

He stops talking for a moment and I hear some noise in the background, but quickly continues.

"They painted symbols on these men, and each symbol summoned different demons. On the day these men were set to come home, the witch doctors put cursed items in their baggage. The chief personally puts two coffins in their belonging, each of which contained a demon…Succubus and me. When he opened my coffin, he released me, and in turn, I released Succubus. Oh, I am sorry…you thought she was on your side? You were right to doubt her, but it was too late to care. Edward thought he could control us, but he was wrong, and he learned that quickly. His darling little girl, Melissa…so young…he misread that message. The message said for him to kill himself and set everything right, but instead he sacrificed his wife and daughter."

A loud bang upstairs interrupts the story, and Dre states, "Ah, I see your friends are done. Edward was too blind to see that all the entire village wanted was for him to kill himself. He got what was coming to him though, an agonizing slow death. Since then, we are here to stay. Thanks to people like you, we've enjoyed ourselves killing you off, one by one. You teenagers are all the same; you always choose to fight rather than just accepting the inevitable fate, which awaits you. This has been a pleasure, Brenda, but now I must make preparations. I must undo some of what you and your friends have done. Don't worry about your friends, I will look after them, you have my word. I hope I do not get too much dirt in your face when I replace these boards. Goodbye Brenda. You put up a good fight; I hope that one day I meet another with your strength."

"Wait…" I whisper, the sound barely making it past my lips.

"What?"

I take a couple of breaths before I respond, "What is going to happen to me?"

"I'll answer that, only because you're a worthy adversary, Brenda. Once Abrazz's moon sits in the sky, or I guess you would know it better as a harvest moon, you'll be protecting this house. Actually, you'll have a second purpose as well. The reason we need you over this well is because it leads to hell. Every person we kill here fills this well, and the necklace and book placed with you keeps the well open until our brothers and sisters pass through. Thanks to you, and the thousands of other people over the years, the well should be close to being full."

Not wanting any more pain from this demon, I hold my tongue. All I can do is listen as I feel dirt trickling all around me. I hear what sounds like something being dragged on the floor above me as the boards crack under the weight of whatever it is. Then all I can hear is my own breathing, and all I can think about are my friends and family. Everyone wondering where I am, and not knowing is going to be the worst. I want to scream at the top of my lungs, but only scream in my head. The pain is overwhelming as I try to move off this plank to fall to what I hope would be my death. I can't even tell if I am moving or not.

Getting ready.

Watching as the dead teens clean up the yard as the rain continues to fall, the vehicles begin to sink into the ground. I nod in approval as everything becomes as it was before the party began last night.

Turning around as Dre comes walking out of the house, he asks, "did you take care of Patricia?"

"I did. We are incessantly united. Patricia offered little resistance, and her enthusiasm was great," I exclaim, smiling as her last moments of bliss cross my mind.

Dre laughs as he replies, "I can't say Brenda's energy was quite as enthusiastic, but now we will just wait and see if anyone finds her before she becomes a skeletal memory from the adornment of time."

"I know I heard them speaking of others coming tonight. I do hope this is true, as I enjoyed myself last night," I reply holding my hands to my chest.

"As did I. They remained so incredibly easy to manipulate. All the things we did to them, and they still stuck around for more."

"Oh yes. Making these teenagers believe there was no place for them to go with you standing out there. That was the greatest moment, watching them try to figure out a way to leave here," I exclaim, laughing.

"It was unbelievable. We must rework this book once again; perhaps we should add a little more? Perhaps we should give them clearer hints as to where to look?"

"Yes, we should. It seemed to take them quite a while to figure some of these things out," I reply, shaking my head, as Dre looks on.

"Indeed, Brenda was kind of interesting. The way she tried her best, the way she broke when all of her friends told her it was her fault they were dead. That was great. And then when she came back with that coffin. You know, she was a smart one; she almost had me a couple of times last night. Like when she actually got me in that coffin... I was sure she wanted me death, but then BAM... she had me. Maybe people will start coming around more."

"Yes, she was smart. A lot smarter than most of them. That Joe was kind of interesting too. Even after I told them he was no good to go out and get you, they still backed his decision to get you in the coffin. That was the greatest moment I ever saw. 'I can do it on one leg.' The way you played with him for a while, that was priceless in itself."

"What about that Cindy? The one you possessed? Is there anything interesting about her we could use?"

"Maybe. Cindy does have a dark side. Not that she plays in the dark arts. She is more to gain the knowledge about what people are about," I reply.

"Yes, maybe we can use that. Once our minions get these boxes back down into the basement, we'll be ready for others," Dre states.

"This time I am going to love making these one's scream like never before. I'll give all the boys everything they have ever wanted," I howl with laughter.

Dre laughs just as hard, as he replies, "Succubus. Yes, you are going to love those boys to death… literally."

"You, Dre, are just going to go about killing them one by one like always. There's no love in the way you do it," I reply, watching as Dre pulls his claws out.

"You got that right. I just want love, and all these teens feeling the pain of death. Whereas you just want to fuck them. I am so glad the chief joined our caskets together to complete this endeavor against Mr. Robinson."

"Yes. Together we hold the world in our hands. The two things people must do: have sex and die. The two things that make it so easy for us," I reply running my hands down my sides.

Dre looks over at me and responds, "Truly one of the greatest moments of our time. So much easier than it used to be. I can still remember the first time… it almost feels like yesterday."

Unhallowed

"Oh yes. I molested Mr. Robinson day and night, and after, I killed that prostitute and made him believe he did it. It drove him insane, and you made sure his fear was realized," I reply, smiling at the memory of those days.

"Your love tormented him for a long time. You did it so well and made it so easy for me to kill him."

"The more people that come here, the faster we can fill up that well. Then we will be unstoppable. We will ravage the lands; we will entomb the world leaders. We will become the world," I state, happily.

Dre nods in agreement, "yes. We will rise to a new world. People will look upon us with admiration, and those who do not admire us will pay with their lives. I cannot wait for that well to flood over so our brothers and sisters may come and go without being summoned."

"That will be a beautiful day. Watching the world become ours. Those vehicles are mostly submerged into the ground, and soon we will be ready."

"The book has rewritten itself, and, decided what secrets it wanted on its pages."

"Excellent. When the people come, their intrigue in the written words will be what condemns them to us. Let us return to our places, and when they arrive, we shall make their short stay here one they will remember for the rest of their lives… no matter how long or short that may be," Dre cackles.

Yes. I shall return to the weed fields and wait for an unsuspecting man, or woman, to come indulge in my wares," I reply, laughing as the thought.

I walk into the weeds towards the willow tree, the rains stop, and the ground begins to dry uncharacteristically quick, returning to crusty dry dirt as if it had never rained in months. As I sit perched in the tree, glancing around, there are none of the vehicles from last night in sight. The house on the prairies looks as if it's been abandoned for years. As evening approaches and new vehicles make their way down the road, coming towards the house, I smile as my thoughts dance around. Who knows what this night will bring...?"

The End

Unhallowed
Synopsis

Brenda is invited to a party at an old abandoned farmhouse just a mere twenty miles west of Saskatoon. The party starts great, and as the circular fire roars, everyone is having fun. As darkness falls over the land, it turns out unknown beings have a different kind of party planned - a party to die for! Brenda and her friends soon find themselves trapped in the little house, trying to find a way to outsmart these spawns of hell. Dre is hell bent on picking off her friends one by one. By morning light, Succubus offers to help Brenda and the few friends she has left. Making the choice between living and dying, Brenda chooses to listen to Succubus and she watches as more of her friends die trying to lock Dre back up in his casket. Brenda finally locks Dre away, but is bleeding to death. Patricia tries to help her, but Succubus makes Patricia an offer she can't refuse. Brenda comes to learn a horrible secret, one that will leave her in the dark... forever.

Don. P. Pankratz
About the author

Don is an avid paranormal enthusiast, and enjoys writing about the many possibly outcomes for ghosts intertwining with the living. Having only started writing in 2013, he has made great strides to provide enjoyable fictional horror, paranormal stories. Unhallowed is the first of many stories Don has written, with many more to come.